Night Time, || || Dotted Line

by

Katherine Silva

Acknowledgements

Thank you to my support network, a.k.a my family and friends, who listened to all of my many crazy ideas when all I had were random chapters and barely a story. Thank you to my fellow Maine writers, E.J. Fechenda and Kate Cone for your wonderful reading series and for allowing me several opportunities to read parts of this book to willing and engaged audiences. And lastly, to those who travel and are able to often all for the sake of getting outside your comfort zone. Wanderlust is a wonderful thing.

Chapter 1

Spencer opened his eyes to a blackened bedroom just before the phone rang. He glanced at the clock. Three A.M. *Only two hours since I hit the pillow.*

Ring, ring.

Damn it.

He peeled back the covers and tore himself out of bed like a reluctant piece of duct tape from a roll. He opened the bedroom door and sauntered into the main hall. *Who the hell is calling now?* He grabbed the receiver from the hall phone. "Hello?"

"Spence, it's Lydia."

Oh. "Did you just get in?" he asked, stifling a yawn.

"A couple hours ago. Forgot to call you and let you know we'd made it all right."

He cleared his throat. "You do realize you're two hours behind in Dallas, right?"

"Sorry. I figured you'd want to know sooner rather than later."

"It's okay." It wasn't. He leaned in the doorframe to the kitchen. His eyes wandered to the coffee maker next to the sink. He started over to it. "Must have been a long flight." The cord pulled taut a foot from the kitchen counter.

Lydia hummed in agreement. "The movers left the truck

1

parked in our drive way. Stu wanted to get some of the boxes moved in tonight. He's got work in the morning."

Spencer cringed. "Good ole Stu. How is he?" he asked, trying not to grit his teeth.

She didn't pick up on the resentment or at least pretended not to. "Aside from being exhausted, he's good."

"Glad to hear it."

Silence. He twirled the phone cord around his finger. His mouth moved, although no voice left it. *It's different without you here.* It was pointless. It had been different for five years. What use would there be to throw it out there? It would only cause more pain. *And I can't afford to get drunk tonight.*

"You sound tired, Spence," she finally said.

"It's three o'clock in the morning."

"Were you up late working?"

"Yeah, I was getting files together for a deposition tomorrow." He caught himself. "Today."

"I guess I'll let you catch some sleep then."

"Yeah, okay. You, too."

"Goodnight, Spence."

"Good morning, Lydia." He hung up the phone and stared at the coffee maker. "Good morning."

*

"Good morning, sir."

Spencer peered over his newspaper. Standing next to his table in the Starbucks was a woman. *Chestnut hair, big glasses, cute nose, oversized plaid shirt... I'm going with hippie.* He squinted. He didn't recognize her. She was probably talking to someone else. He turned back to the paper.

"Excuse me."

He glanced up again. *Nope, she's talking to me.* He nudged the sugar on the table toward her. "Here you go."

"I don't need that."

"Okay. Did you want the table?"

"My name is Calleigh Royle. I just wanted to ask you a question."

She's too young to be a hippie. Probably late twenties. Parents were probably hippies. What was the term now? Hipster? He looked at his watch. *Deposition is at nine.* "Okay, ask away."

"Next week, there's an environmental conference happening in the Malheur National Forest in Canyon City, Oregon."

The words bounded past his ears. *What is this bullshit?* "Okay."

"I'm looking for someone to go with me out there."

Spencer folded the newspaper, his brows furrowing. "Are you asking if I know anyone who wants to go?"

"I was asking if you wanted to go."

"Then why didn't you just ask?"

"I did."

Hmm, young and smart-mouthed. "I can't."

3

"Why not?"

"Because I've got a job. Just like I'm sure most of the other people in this coffee shop do." He put the newspaper between them again. "Put an ad in the paper."

"It's too late for that."

Why isn't she going away? "That's your problem not mine."

She cleared her throat.

Okay, now she's mad and she's not going away. Hope she isn't a murderous psychopath or something. "Put up a notice on the corkboard over there," he suggested.

She scraped the chair out across from him and sat. "What do you do for a living?"

Oh, great. Now she wants to play twenty questions. "I'm a lawyer."

She scoffed "Should have figured."

"Should have figured I'd have a job? Yeah, that's kind of obvious."

Calleigh plucked a sugar packet from the holder in the middle of the table and tipped it from end to end. "Most people have paid vacations."

"I'm not going to spend mine stuck on the road for two weeks with some tree-hugger I don't even know."

"I'm not a tree-hugger."

"Could have fooled me."

"I'd pay for half the gas."

He put down the paper again, this time nearly taking out his coffee cup by accident. "Listen, lady—"

"Calleigh."

"—Calleigh, why don't you just go alone?"

"I don't have the money to do it alone. If I could split expenses with someone, then I could manage."

"Why don't you just take a flight to Oregon?"

"I'm afraid of flying."

The quicker her responses, the more he felt his annoyance rise. He locked eyes with her. "So, you're asking strangers in a coffee shop if they'll go with you on a spur-of-the-moment, three thousand mile road trip to a tree-hugger's convention?" He took a sip from his cappuccino.

"It isn't a tree-hugging convention," she said. "It's an environmental conference. And yes, statistically speaking, coffee shops are one of the top ten places to meet people. I figured I'd at least give it a shot."

"Did you just refer to dating statistics to make your argument?"

She blew a raspberry. "I didn't come over here to argue. But you *are* a lawyer. It's in your nature to argue so I should have expected it."

"Could you maybe stop talking and please go away?"

She straightened and, with one perked brow, turned and walked to a nearby table, striking up a conversation with the person there.

Spencer groaned as he checked his watch again. *Damn. So*

much for a peaceful morning coffee. He got up from the table and left the Starbucks. He glanced over his shoulder through the big front windows. Calleigh had been rejected by her latest target and was now trying another.

What a loon, he thought as he unlocked his car and climbed in. *Oh well. I'm sure she'll find someone equally as crazy to go with her.*

He waited for a break in the traffic and pulled out onto the road.

*

Spencer watched the second hand swing around the clock face. Just like that, time slid by noiselessly in that little grey room of hell. He'd been there for fifteen minutes staring at the folder in front of him. Across the table, he heard the heavy breathing of his opposing council. He'd had enough of her rolling eyes, heard enough of her tapping fingernails against the glass table. The only other noise was a squirrel chirping on a tree branch outside the window.

Ivy Sherman, a woman of narrow features, thin lips, and small assets sat directly across the table from him. He didn't dare look into her acid green gaze, knowing that to be trapped in it spelled terror. She was known for getting her way, had a near impeccable record at the law offices of Garland and Houston. She straightened the creases in her grey business suit before resuming her tireless nail clicking.

The prosecuting client, Gina Sutton, sat next to her. Lazy and yet tense, she was like an overly fed cat that still thought it could catch a bird swooping by. Her tangled hair was pulled back into a slovenly formed bun. Beneath the surplus of skin on her face, beady black eyes glared across the table at him, a gaze with so much malice it could strangle that squirrel outside if she looked at it the wrong way.

And here he sat, alone on his side, his eyes locked on that clock while his hand, unbeknownst to everyone else, was clenched into a fist beneath the table.

"Should we take a five minute recess so you can call your client, Mr. Teel?" Ivy finally said, her tone sickly sweet like cheap candy.

That unreliable bastard, Spencer thought, pulling the mobile phone out of his pocket. No missed calls. He couldn't say he was surprised though.

His client, Donat LeRoy, was a naturalized citizen originally from France and one of New England's top chefs. Since moving to Maine, he had opened three different restaurants in Bangor, Augusta, and Portland and two in Boston. More recently, he was negotiating a few pieces of property in the mid-west to turn into restaurants as well. The press loved him and frequently ran stories on his achievements. If only their last story had been as positive as earlier ones had been.

After becoming staggeringly drunk one night, LeRoy had managed to not only hit Gina Sutton's car but somehow catch it on fire as well. But, in his drunken stupor, he'd fled the scene of the crime before the authorities arrived. Despite the car being registered to him, there were no eyewitnesses who could say that he was driving it nor did LeRoy own up to the fact himself.

"C'est un voiture d'entreprise…a company car. I loan it out to my employees all de time," he'd said when originally confronted by police. "If I'm zere and zey need to make a run to de market, I give zem de keys. I can't help if one took it for a joyride and destroyed someone's car."

The case had dragged on for months at a time, mostly in lieu of the fact that LeRoy was nearly impossible to keep in contact with. Owning a successful chain of restaurants kept him traveling constantly. The court's wishes and desires were of little importance to him. For all Spencer knew, LeRoy could have flown to Michigan that morning on business, completely uninterested in the idea of a deposition.

He looked back at Ivy and nodded. "I'll give him a call."

*

"Pick up the phone, you son of a bitch," Spencer said under his breath as he paced. He'd gone out to the front of the building for privacy, but mostly to escape that room. The air had grown stale so quickly, it almost felt like being trapped in a submarine underwater. And that stare that Sutton had given him felt just as suffocating. *Good thing I'm not a squirrel.*

The phone went to voicemail. Spencer's mind tumbled with the endless curses he wanted to leave after the beep. But when the time came, he composed himself and said, "Mr. LeRoy, this is Spencer Teel. Not sure if you remembered but the deposition was this morning… Umm…call me when you get this. We need to talk."

He slapped the phone shut just as Ivy walked through the glass doors. In the mid-afternoon sunlight, her short dark hair glimmered with the red highlights. It also bleached her skin out terribly. *When was the last time she saw the sun?*

"Did you get through to Mr. LeRoy?" she asked but the answer was already in her tone. She knew he hadn't.

Spencer straightened and, in spite of himself, pulled at the collar of his shirt. "No. He must have forgotten."

"Your client seems to forget things often," Ivy said, the charm all but gone from her voice. "This is the second deposition he's failed to show up at."

Heat swelled as the sun glared down over them. He felt beads of sweat beginning to form along the back of his neck. "I realize that. As you know, Mr. LeRoy has many obligations to his business."

"As a citizen of this country, he has obligations to the law," Ivy growled. "Or did he not understand that when he promised to uphold and obey the laws in that oath he was given?"

Spencer pulled at his collar again. The temperature spiked. "Can we talk more about this after we've adjourned the deposition?"

"I think it's worth discussing, yes," she clipped as she turned her back on him and started back into the building.

Wouldn't want you to burst into flames from all that sunlight, would we?

He started after her. The shadows of the building slid over him and a blast of cold wind from the air-conditioner slapped him in the face.

Ivy turned back toward him as they neared the elevator. "Don't think I'm letting you off the hook."

He nodded if only to get her attention off him for a second. He glanced down at his hand. It trembled. He forced it into his pocket as the elevator doors opened and they both got inside.

In that cramped space, the heat swarmed all around him again. *Haven't had one of these attacks in weeks,* he thought, leaning against the back of the box. The ceiling and floor seemed to tilt toward one another. Even tucked in the confines of his pants pocket, Spencer couldn't keep his hand still. It jittered on its own, completely out of his control.

Ivy watched him out of the corner of her eyes.

Don't say anything. You didn't see anything.

She didn't. But he knew she'd noticed. Maybe she didn't care enough. Either way, it was awkward. As the elevator climbed, he felt the heat growing and rising. He reached into his jacket pocket and his fingers rubbed over the bottle of pills there. He needed one. He knew he wouldn't be able to make it through the rest of the meeting without one.

The elevator pinged and the doors opened. Ivy stalked out ahead of him.

"I'll be there in a second." he said, darting toward the bathrooms.

She turned to argue but wasn't fast enough before he'd ducked into the men's room. At the sink, he opened the bottle and swallowed one pill roughly. Turning the water on full blast, he scooped it into his mouth, then splashed his face. *Pull yourself together.*

He watched his hand silently for a moment. *What am I doing here?* he thought. He focused on his ring finger and the band of lighter skin where a wedding ring used to be. *Divorced, living in an apartment I can hardly pay for. I'm getting cases which I keep losing... And then this.* After another few moments, he'd stilled it enough so that he could walk into that office without worry of anyone really noticing. Then, he left the bathroom.

As he made his way down the hall, his thoughts fell back on the coffee shop that morning and the peculiar woman there, Calleigh. In a strange way, he'd actually enjoyed the argument between them. She'd been quick with an answer at every question. She'd been quirky, sure, but there was something about her that seemed oddly likeable. It had been a long time since he'd had a conversation much less a quarrel like that with anyone. He didn't even realize that he was smiling when he pushed through the door into the conference room.

Ivy was still seething but there was curiosity in her gaze as well. He didn't like it. "Everything all right?" Her tone was cheeky.

He gave her a direct gaze. "Peachy. Thanks for asking."

*

Part of him figured that Calleigh had found someone to go with her on her bizarre cross-country journey to the conference. After all, if she'd spent the entire day downtown shopping around for a road-trip buddy, she was likely to come across some vegan snob or a college-age environmentalist stooge with nothing better to do. But an even smaller sliver of him, the sliver that had caused him to go back to the Starbucks that evening, had expected, even hoped to see her still there.

As he approached, he saw her sitting at one of the tables in the corner. A half-empty paper cup sat on the table in front of her along with her glasses. She looked exhausted and in her face, he also read defeat.

Why am I doing this? He considered to himself as he slowed to a stop in front of the doors. *Have I really lost it? Am I having a mid-life crisis?*

He stared at her.

Maybe.

She turned and noticed him, perking up.

I could be a jerk and walk away. She doesn't have to know what I was here for.

He pushed open the door despite of the marathon of excuses now in his head and walked to the counter. "Coffee, black," he told the acne-scarred kid at the register. He cautiously looked at Calleigh. She was still staring at him.

"You're still here?" he asked her, handing the kid his credit card.

She chuckled. "You knew I'd be."

"I don't know what you're talking about. I come here every night after work."

"Where's your briefcase?"

"It's in the car."

She arched an eyebrow. "Why not just make your own coffee at home? You could save a few bucks."

"I like this coffee better."

Stupid answer, he thought as he watched her smirk. *She knows.*

He collected his coffee and took a small sip. *Get out of here while you still can. It's not too late to salvage your career.*

"Have you thought anymore about my offer?" Calleigh asked, breaking him out of his train-of-thought.

He moved toward her table even though his mind told him to go the opposite way. "I still think it's crazy."

"Of course it's crazy." She picked up her glasses from the table and started rubbing the lenses. "That's what makes it fun."

Despite not having an invitation to join her, he sat opposite her. "What's so special about this trip? Why do you have to do this?"

"Does it have to be special? Does there really need to be a ground-breaking reason?"

"It just seems like it's really important to you, that's all."

She was quiet and she stared down at her own coffee cup. For a few moments, he thought he'd actually stumped her and his success gave way to a sort of disappointment. *I really have lost my mind...*

Then she said it. "It's just something that I have to do. Haven't you ever had something you just had to do? And it didn't matter what anyone said about it, you wouldn't change your mind."

"Maybe when I was a kid," Spencer answered. "But I don't get to make choices that freely anymore. I've got obligations now. I can't just do what I want."

"Can't you?"

"I—"

She gazed at him in such a way that he realized she was right. The only reason he was sitting there was because he'd wanted a change of some sort, not just engaging Calleigh's challenging personality but actually needed something to break this monotonous routine he'd fallen into.

"Tell me something," Calleigh continued, "did you come here so that I could talk you out of going? Or so I could talk you into it?"

All he could picture in his head was Lydia, tanning on the back deck to some new development in Texas with Stu beside her, a grin on his face that just oozed pleasure.

He took a giant slug of his coffee and nodded. "When do we leave?

Chapter 2

Spencer drove his Lexus along the streets of Midcoast Maine at seven o'clock the next morning. The sun had come up only an hour ago. As he rounded a deep blue lake, he watched the sky above, a dome of clear blue with high wispy clouds. He'd never really bothered to watch it before. Everything that mattered to him was on the Earth. But just for the first time in a very long time, he noticed the sky. It concaved above him. He suddenly had the feeling as if he was inside an eggshell. It was a feeling he'd never had before, a feeling that seemed to diminish any grand feelings he'd had about this journey ahead. He was suddenly miniature in those moments. He wasn't sure he liked that.

The road ahead of him dipped down a hill into a town. As he neared an intersection, he pulled over to the side of the road and double-checked the directions he'd received from Calliegh. This was the place. His sunglasses slid down his nose as he gazed at the house.

It was a two-story pale green house with forest green shutters, a wrap-around porch and a cross-gabled roof. There were only two cars in the driveway. One was a small red Nissan that appeared to have been well-used. Its passenger side mirror was missing and it was speckled with mud. The other car didn't look much better. The

Studebaker Wagonaire's front end was propped up on blocks; the hood opened up and front tires missing. He winced. *Please tell me neither of these are her car. Tell me her car's in a garage somewhere off premises.*

He pulled his Lexus into the driveway behind the Studebaker and turned it off. Then, jumping out, he climbed the stairs up to the porch, found the door to Calleigh's apartment, 6A, and knocked on it. Something shattered inside.

"Shit!" Calleigh called out from somewhere upstairs. Barking erupted from a room at the back of the apartment. *I really am crazy,* Spencer realized moments before the door opened.

Calleigh grinned as she saw him. "Hey! You're a little early."

Spencer checked his watch. "So I am. Sorry if I…startled you."

She glanced back over her shoulder and chuckled nervously. "It was just a pitcher. Not one of my favorites."

A little body squirmed out by her legs and leapt up at Spencer. He took a few steps back. The Corgi stood on its hind legs and just barely came up to Spencer's torso. Its large ears pricked up in excitement, and it started barking all the louder. Its little legs looked barely able to support its overweight belly.

"Ah, this is Newton," she said, giving the dog's head an affectionate rub.

He looked down at the animal. *It isn't a dog. It's a sausage with legs.* "Newton? As in 'fig newton?'"

"As in 'Isaac Newton'. You know, the guy who discovered

16

gravity." She glared, picking up the dog and holding him.

"Yeah, gravity. You couldn't have picked a more perfect name."

She sighed and put the dog back inside. "If you want to wait outside, I'll just be another minute. I've got to grab a couple more things." She paused before she added, "Or you can come in if you want."

The thought of standing outside on the porch was shot down in a moment. The humidity had already climbed unbearably since he'd gotten in his car that morning. "I had to peel myself out of the driver's seat a few minutes ago. I'll wait inside." He followed her through the door.

Spencer pulled off his sunglasses and let his eyes to adjust to the dusky interior. There were thin curtains over most of the windows and though they didn't completely block out the sunlight, they cut the temperature down quite a bit.

The furniture was rustic. A lot of it looked like it had been salvaged from thrift stores and estate sales, judging by the fabric patterns. He glanced at an upholstered loveseat in the living room with hot pink and orange geometric patterns dotting it. *So this is where the 60's went.* An assortment of plants had all been pushed around the one window on the eastern wall. *Wonder who's going to take care of those while we're gone.*

Newton waddled in from the kitchen and sat down on Spencer's shoe, opening his jaws into a giant yawn. Spencer frowned.

Not to mention who's going to take care of Gravitron here.

He carefully slid his shoe out from under the dog and turned toward the kitchen. "So, I couldn't help noticing the old car in the parking lot," he called up the stairs to Calleigh

"You mean the Studebaker? Yeah, it's my neighbor's. It's been a project of his to get it running for a few years now."

"Seems like a lost cause. Why not just buy a new car?" He peeked in the kitchen. *Tidy.* He glanced down at the dog's water bowl and food dish. When he took a step back he heard the crunch of dog kibble under his shoe. *Tidy-ish.*

"I don't know. Nostalgia? It gives him something to do. I think he needs a project like that."

"I have to admit, I was a little worried when I got here. I thought it might have been your car."

She chuckled. "No. The Nissan is my road rambler; gets me where I want to go in no time."

Damn. "How old is it?"

"I think it's a '94. It's lasted pretty well, considering..."

"Considering what?"

"That the alternator has gone three times in it and I had to replace the battery again last month."

He returned to the bottom of the stairs. "You know, maybe we could take my car."

"Oh, you mean the gas guzzler you drove in here?"

"It's not a gas guzzler!"

A door closed upstairs. "How many miles to the gallon *does* it get?"

"Eighteen…maybe nineteen." He'd never really thought about it before. He'd bought the car back several years ago when things had been going well for him. At that time, he hadn't cared about saving money. He was making enough as it was. Besides, he needed a new car and he wanted one that would be reliable. "I didn't buy it for its gas efficiency though."

"Why did you buy it?"

He felt something warm tickling his fingers. He looked down. Newton was licking them. He pulled his hand away. "It's a Lexus. Why do you think I bought it?"

"Because you're ostentatious?"

He laughed. "If you knew me, you'd know that's far from the truth."

She clomped down the stairs with a duffel bag slung over one shoulder and a backpack over the other. She dropped them on the floor with a heavy thud and pushed by him into the kitchen.

"Geez, what'd you put in there? The Library of Congress?"

"I've got some camping supplies just in case we end up needing to pitch a tent at some point." She disappeared into her pantry. "My car might be excellent on mileage but it's not the most comfortable thing to spend the night in."

"'Pitch a tent?' I assumed we'd be staying at motels the whole way?"

"If you want to run out of money before we get to Oregon, then we can." She scoffed as she came back out into view with several packages of dehydrated and canned food. "I don't mind spending a couple nights out under the stars if you don't. We'll be camping when we get to the park anyway."

He frowned, realizing there was a slight tremor in his hand. He crossed his arms, hoping she hadn't noticed. "I might stay in the car anyway."

She unzipped the bag and stuffed the food in. "You aren't very outdoorsy, are you?"

"I can handle the great outdoors for a couple nights," he said, leaning against the wall near the stairs. "I just haven't been camping outside of a campground since I was ten."

She chuckled. "You were once a kid?" She put a hand to her heart. "Shocking!"

"We spent the day fishing, looking for animal tracks in the woods… That night, we had a campfire."

"And cooked the fish you caught?"

"We didn't catch any," he said, staring down at the floor. "I scared them all away by shouting about how I couldn't catch any. Patience wasn't in my vocabulary."

Calleigh smiled. "Imagine that."

He shot her a cheerless grin. "Funny!"

"I thought so."

"Anyway, that night, I woke up to a family of earwigs crawling on my face." He shuddered.

Calleigh finished packing and stood up. "That one bad experience kept you from trying it again?"

"We stuck to day trips after that."

She whistled. Newton came tottering in from another room, panting heavily. She reached for the leash hanging on a rack by the door.

"Wait, you're bringing the dog?"

"Well, I can't just leave him here," she said as if it were a joke and clipped the leash to Newton's collar.

"Isn't there anyone who can take care of him?" He pointed to the living room. "Maybe the same person who's going to take care of your rainforest in there."

Calleigh narrowed her eyes at him. "Do you have a problem with dogs?"

"No, I just—"

"Newton and I have been inseparable since I got him. Plus he has high anxiety. If I left him here while I went cross-country for two weeks, he'd have a panic attack."

"Have you tried sitting him down with a therapist, try to talk through some of those coddling issues…"

She shot him a glare. "He's coming with us."

Great, Spencer thought. "You know a lot of motels don't allow pets."

"You'd be surprised at how flexible some motels can be." She hoisted her backpack onto her shoulder and opened the front door. She turned back to look at the duffel bag, then at him. "Mind getting that?"

"No problem, Cleopatra." He picked it up and suddenly felt akin to a weightlifter hoisting up a hundred pound barbell.

The heat slapped him as soon as he was through the door. The sun had risen higher in the sky and beat down on them with merciless intensity. He dropped her duffel into the open trunk of the Nissan and returned to the Lexus to grab his stuff.

Calleigh's face slackened as she saw his one bag. "That's it?"

"Forgive me if I didn't bring all the clothes in my closet."

"You don't look like you brought very much at all."

"I've got the essentials. That's all that matters."

She cocked her head as she rolled down the back door windows. "Okay. Hope you like wearing the same thing three days in a row."

He scoffed as he climbed into the front passenger seat and shut the door. He used to travel a lot a few years back. He used to taking red-eyes across the country with only the clothes on his back and the litigation papers in his backpack. He could handle this.

Calleigh heaved Newton into the backseat and shut the door before joining Spencer up front. "All right, here we go!"

The car started up with a choked rumble. Spencer's self-confidence faltered. *The car'll probably croak before we've left Maine,* he thought as they backed out of the driveway and began down the road.

*

Within the first hour, Spencer knew it was going to be a long trip. Calleigh had talked incessantly for twenty minutes about some of the seminars she wanted to attend at the conference when they reached it. For some reason, it hadn't occurred to him to look up the place on the internet the night before. He'd spent zero time thinking about what he would do when he got there, only the journey ahead of them.

Environmental conferences were something he knew still happened but had always figured were on a smaller scale: a group of fifty, maybe a hundred people gathered in some dilapidated camp out in the woods, getting in touch with Mother Nature. Most of them were people who hadn't outgrown the sixties, buying free love with as many drugs as one could take. Alternatively, it was a group of twenty-something kids, all too young to really understand the matter but old enough to think they did and have an attitude about it. These "conferences" usually went either one way or another, polar opposites. They'd paint some crude signs and stand on a sidewalk outside some corporate building, shouting like howler monkeys. Or, they'd spend their time sitting in a remote area of the forest, grieving to the trees about how they've been treated. What would this be like?

They drove past Damariscotta following Route 1 toward Wiscassett. It was climbing into the nineties. The conifers stood tall and unmoving, not a hint of a breeze in sight. Despite this, Calleigh had rolled all the windows down instead of hitting the air-conditioner ("To save gas," she'd said). The surge of air roared in his ears, blocking out most of what she'd said.

Newton was perched in the window behind Spencer's head. Every once in a while, he'd hear the jingle of the license on the collar and heavy panting as the dog switched to the other window.

The car bumped onto the Wiscassett Bridge and the fresh taste of the sea spilled into the car. He used to hate this bridge because it was always a guaranteed gridlock spot. Rush hour times of eight o'clock a.m. and five o'clock p.m. were the worst. Knowing about them wasn't enough to avoid getting stuck in them while trying to get to the airport for a last minute flight. He'd end up in a line that stretched three quarters of a mile down Route 1. One by one, each car would thump over the railroad tracks on the opposite side of the bridge and crawl up the steep hill through town, making sure to stop for pedestrians who always seemed to materialize out of thin air. They'd missed that rush this morning, thankfully.

As Calleigh negotiated through the rollercoaster-esque turns in the road, Newton suddenly plunged headlong into Spencer's lap, scraping his claws to get to the open window.

"God!"

"Newton, get in the back!" Calleigh ordered through a grin that she tried to hide.

The dog stood up on Spencer's legs and propped his front paws on the window, his tongue flapping in the breeze.

"His English might be a little rusty," Spencer remarked, wrapping his hands around Newton's middle and hefting him into the

24

back seat with a grunt.

"I take it you don't have any pets," Calleigh said.

Spencer could tell she was having a hard time wiping that smile off her face. He wondered if she'd made up that stuff about Newton having a high anxiety just so she'd have an excuse to bring him. "I don't."

"Any particular reason?"

"I'm not home enough of the time. Also, the apartment isn't animal friendly. I don't think my landlord would allow it." He didn't have to think about that. He *knew* he wouldn't.

She veered the car through a series of turns. "Not even a goldfish?"

His childhood came back to haunt him with those words. "I'm pretty sure I hold the world record for inadvertent goldfish kills."

Calleigh scoffed. "Oh, come on."

"Ever since the last one, my parents didn't trust me with any other pets."

"So you're telling me that a dead fish kept you from owning any other pets your entire life?"

"No. Well, technically, I had one. My ex-wife had a cat."

"Oh." He noticed Calleigh's eyes widen behind the brown lenses of her over-sized sunglasses. "Ex-wife?"

"Recent."

"Still bitter about it, huh?"

"That topic is off-limits," he added quickly.

"Fine. So about the cat…?"

"Daffodil was its name. In the apartment we used to keep, it liked to hang out in the bathroom. I'd go in there to shave and lo and behold, there was Daffodil sound asleep in the sink."

"I'm surprised you didn't shave the cat."

"Oh, I was tempted."

She chuckled. "When I was little, my parents had a cat that slept in the sink."

"Daffodil was also extremely territorial. She'd pee on everything I owned. My briefcase, my running shoes, even on the bathmat once while I was in the shower…"

Calleigh clicked her tongue. "Guess you were happy to be rid of the cat when the divorce went through, huh?"

"The cat was gone long before we ever talked about a divorce. She choked on a chicken bone and died."

Calleigh eyed him. "You slipped it in with her wet food, didn't you?"

"God, if I'd done that, it would have been way funnier than it actually was. Lydia cried for days."

Calleigh took a deep breath. "Well, this conversation went a lot more morbidly than I'd intended."

"Just goes to show that you can't judge future traveling companions based on how they seem in a coffee shop," he said.

"Oh, believe me, if our conversation then was enough to go on, I'd have been able to judge."

He wagged a finger at her. "Judging a book by its cover doesn't count."

She glanced at him out of the corner of her eyes. "I said "if"."

*

Calleigh pulled the Nissan off into a rest area two hours later, grabbed Newton from the back seat and clipped his leash on.

Spencer frowned. "I knew we'd never get out of Maine."

Calleigh ignored him. "I'm taking Newton for a walk."

Spencer climbed out of the car and gasped from the still oppressive heat. He started toward the rest stop building.

"Hey!"

He turned back to Calleigh.

"Mind getting me a coffee while you're in there?"

"Mind putting on the A/C when we get back in the car?" he countered.

She squinted as if she was considering which was more important; coffee or winning the "green" argument that he was sure would continue for the rest of the trip. She finally gave in. "Fine."

Once he'd finished in the bathroom inside, he went to the convenience store and dispensed two iced coffees and nabbed a small packet of aspirin. He had a feeling he was going to need it. The air conditioning was on inside and it was a welcome relief from that toaster box of a car.

Do I really have to go back out?

He gazed around the rest stop, focusing on the chorus of

coughing coming from a family with four kids sitting in the McDonald's, all screaming and fighting over their toys. He focused on the tourists in line at the donut shop in their uniform morning grogginess. And, of course, there were those sketchy people that hung around the outside of the bathrooms. They never went inside nor were ever waiting for anyone to come out. They just stood there and stood there.

Nope, he decided. *I'm leaving.*

He pushed out the front doors with his back. Calleigh and Newton were in a fenced-off area across the parking lot. There was an older woman with her border collie walking on the opposite side of the enclosure. Spencer closed in on Calleigh and handed her coffee over the chain-link fence.

"Thanks!" She took a large gulp and promptly spit it out. "How much sugar did you put in this?"

"I figured you liked your coffee light and sweet."

She blew a raspberry. "Black."

"Oh."

"And I never said I wanted iced."

"Well, seeing as how it's ninety degrees, I figured it made sense."

She looked up toward the sky. "Hot, black coffee. It does the trick every morning."

"If you want to spontaneously combust…"

She reached over the fence, and took a swipe at his coffee cup.

"What's yours?"

He lifted it up out of her reach. "It's still iced. One sugar, one cream and no, you can't have it."

Calleigh sighed as she let Newton lead her along the fence line. She took another sip from her coffee and cringed as she swallowed.

Spencer followed outside the fence. "So, on this trip, are we going to have to stop every two hours to walk the dog?"

"I don't know. You think we should stop every time *you* need to pee?"

"I don't pee every two hours."

"Neither does the dog," she said. "And thanks for telling me how often you pee. That was vital for me to know."

He rolled his eyes and sat down on a nearby bench. "If we stop every few hours, where do you think we'll get by the end of the day today?"

"I was hoping for New York," she called back to him.

"Tut. If we make it off the Mass Pike, it'll be a miracle."

Calleigh circled back, her sunglasses sliding down her nose. "I've made a day's drive to Upstate New York before."

"With the dog?"

"Yes."

"Just you and the dog?"

"No," she said but didn't elaborate. Spencer thought he detected a shift in her cocky attitude, like walls going up. It was gone before he could question it further.

"We'd better be moving on. We've still got a lot of road ahead of us," Calleigh said, unlatching the fence door and practically towing Newton along. The dog whined as the grassy romping ground was left behind and he was placed back in the car. Spencer felt much of the same sadness of returning to it.

Calleigh started the engine and began backing out of their space.

"Hang on." Spencer glanced at her window. "You promised."

She exhaled as she rolled up the window and Spencer did the same with his. When she flipped the switch on the dash for the A/C, warm stale air blasted from the vents. It smelled of old dog hair and mildew and probably hadn't been used in over a year. He suddenly wondered if he'd changed his mind about doing this entire trip.

Calleigh looked behind her as she backed out of the space and slowly drove down toward the pull-out lane that would put them back on the interstate.

"You know what? Nevermind," Spencer said, flipping off the A/C and rolling his window back down.

"We made a deal," she answered, although she didn't seem upset at all to have the fresh outside air back in the car.

He stared out the window toward the thick forest of evergreens that stood beyond the rest stop. "I brought you the wrong kind of coffee," was all he said.

Chapter 3

It wasn't too much longer before the car was crossing the Piscataqua River Bridge into New Hampshire. It was in this moment that the journey ahead suddenly became real to Spencer. Until then, it had felt like a game with the verbal swordplay against Calleigh, particularly the little nitpicks about the car and the dog and his ex-wife's cat and the coffee... But now, it was different. Somehow, he enjoyed it. *This is good*, he thought. This thought stayed with him as he and Calleigh chit-chatted through New Hampshire on the benefits and mutual love of coffee. When they hit the Mass Pike, all of that positive anticipation evaporated and became a transformed anger.

Spencer had driven the Mass Pike many times and never was there a time that he'd actually enjoyed it. Most often, he was traveling down to Boston and ended up being caught in the snarls of traffic just outside the city. The few times he drove the length of Massachusetts following I-90 were the most strenuous though. It was usually a three to four hour journey wherein he was bound to get caught up in construction, inadvertent traffic backups, and often times, had to contend with some of the most aggressive drivers on the planet.

After an hour of being on I-90, he noticed the sky had darkened considerably. Spencer stared up at the black thunderheads that had taken over. "Great," he grumbled, leaning back in his seat. "Hope this thing floats because it looks like we're about to get a lot of rain."

Calleigh only hummed in agreement. The steep cliff-sides and green forests on either side of them soon gave way to slick glass towers and metal warehouses. Embankments rose up on both sides of the highway near the last of the woodland. Just as they'd left it behind and entered the city, lightening cracked ahead.

Newton's wedge-shaped head popped up in the space between Spencer's and Calleigh's seats. He whimpered.

Calleigh lightly pushed his head into the backseat. "It's okay, boy."

They followed the slowly clotting traffic through the bends in the turnpike. Scores of billboards posted atop the buildings advertised everything from hotels to baked beans and condoms. Motels littered the city with their little rotating signs sticking up like toothpicks.

Thunder rumbled directly overhead and Spencer twitched. The dog let out a shrill bark.

"Newton, it's okay. Calm down," Calleigh whispered.

"What? Does he have a thing about storms?"

"He hates them. Ever since I got him from the shelter, he's been like this," she said. "He was in the dog cell closest to the window. They had a lightning rod attached to their storage shed at the shelter and I'm sure he must have seen lightning strike it plenty of times while he was there."

Spencer looked over his shoulder at the dog. He was turning around in circles. It immediately reminded him of what his ex-wife's

32

cat used to do when it was about to lie down. Except that Newton never lied down. He just kept spinning around like a three year old trying to make himself dizzy.

Rain began to fall a few minutes later. It didn't take long for it to turn into a downpour. Water pounded on the car like thousands of drums. It seemed as though not just Spencer's, but also Calleigh's tension level spiked immediately when it did. He closed his eyes and tried to drown out the sounds with thoughts of work, thoughts of his office, his apartment, his last morning run, anything to take himself out of that car.

Then, Calleigh muttered, "Oh no."

Spencer opened his eyes. He had to squint to see through the glass with all of the runoff but soon, he understood what she meant. There was a hazy yellow light blinking up ahead. Trickling down from it stretched four jam-packed lanes of cars. Soon enough, they were stopped along with them.

"Must have been an accident or something," she said, trying to see past the car in front of her. "That's got to be it."

"You're making me feel better already," Spencer answered.

The steady stream of water suddenly sounded much closer. Only when he turned around did he realize that it wasn't coming from outside the car. "Calleigh! Your dog!"

Newton had whizzed all over the floor on the passenger side behind him. When the dog was done, he leapt up onto the backseat and rolled over onto his back, his tail tucked between his chubby hind legs.

"He's scared. He didn't mean it," she said sympathetically. She reached back to rub the dog's head but couldn't quite reach it. The car in front of her inched forward a little. She stopped trying to pet Newton when the car behind her honked.

She righted herself in the driver's seat and pulled forward the required foot and a half. "There," she said in her rearview mirror at the driver, her teeth gritted. "You happy now?"

The dog whimpered and stood, resuming his spinning motion.

The Nissan inched along the highway for another twenty minutes. Every time there was a hint of movement ahead, the car behind would begin blasting its horn obnoxiously. Calleigh muttered under her breath as she glared back at it through her mirror. Spencer could tell she was going to explode at any moment. He would have, too, if he'd been driving.

He stared at the line up ahead. They were now close enough so they could see what had happened. A tractor trailer had careened off the road toward the midway and struck the guard rail separating the north and south bound lanes. It had tipped and dumped its cargo. A bunch of steel pipes lay scattered across the road. It was going to take a long time to clean everything up; several hours anyway.

The lightning storm hadn't let up either. It was so dark out that it might as well have been night. Every time there was a flash of white light, Newton would scramble around the backseat furiously, yipping and howling.

Spencer closed his eyes, feeling his own anxiety rising. His hand had begun shaking. He was hoping he could avoid taking any pills in front of Calleigh, and this wasn't the place to have an episode. He slid his hand out of view just as she looked his way.

Calleigh put a hand to her forehead. "Guess we won't be getting as far as I'd planned today."

The car behind her started honking again.

"I can't move, you jerkoff!" she screamed.

Newton whined and jumped down behind her seat.

She sighed. "I don't know how much more of this I can take."

Spencer clicked his seatbelt and felt it slither off his lap. Turning in his seat, he reached back and grabbed the dog's midsection. Newton didn't struggle, only went limp like some kind of gigantic slug. He pulled him up into his lap and eased him down into a sitting position. Then, he gently rubbed the dog's chest in circular motions with his fingers.

When Spencer looked up at Calleigh, she was staring at him. "What are you doing?"

"I'm not sure."

"Then why—"

"Gimme a minute."

Newton was leaning forward into his touch, though still whining. Thunder boomed over the car and Spencer felt him shift.

The cars all moved and with a chorus of honking, Calleigh eased the Nissan up to join them. "Now if only we could get that moron to stop honking," she said.

"Do you have any music we could put on?"

She blinked. "Yeah. Hang on." She clicked on the radio. Banging guitar pulsed over the speakers accompanied by a reverberating bass. Newton barked excitedly and squirmed in Spencer's arms.

"Something calm!"

Calleigh flicked it to an indie station. Ray LaMontagne played over the low flickers of static in the background.

"We all need to take a breath here," he said, stroking the dog's fuzzy chest again. "We're getting way too worked up over this."

Calleigh scoffed. "Never took you for the calm guru type."

"I'm not."

He recognized the question in her gaze but she didn't follow it any further. Instead, the silence was cut through by the honking from the car behind them. Calleigh opened her mouth.

"Don't," Spencer interrupted. "What good is it going to do? Shouting only upsets the dog. I don't want to be swimming in a sea of dog pee by the time this car ride is over. Do you?"

That made her shut up. She kept her hands on the wheel and her eyes on the blurry road ahead.

The rain pounded on the roof of the car. Inside, locked in the pleasant slow harmony of the song and eyes watching the fuzzy red of tail lights in front of them, Spencer felt Newton settle into his lap. As he did, his own tension gave way. He took a deep breath.

Calleigh seemed to follow him as if he were a breathing coach, inhaling and exhaling after he did. For some reason, it made her seem more child-like as if she really didn't know what to do in this kind of situation. He began to wonder how she'd ever done a trip like this before. Even to New York, he thought she must have blown a gasket more than enough times with the way she'd just reacted. That is, if she'd driven alone… He couldn't pass up the thought that she was keeping something from him. But now wasn't the time to bring that up. They were making progress.

They were able to pass by the wreck within the next half hour and after another mile or so of gridlocked traffic, the lanes opened up and they were once again free. The downpour continued for the next couple hours. Calleigh kept the car under fifty, still barely able to see out the windshield. Newton retreated to the backseat and sacked out within moments of doing so.

Four o'clock saw the rain lighten a little. A bluish hue could be seen on the horizon far off. They stopped at a rest stop and after devouring a couple of veggie wraps and chips, Spencer took the wheel.

Being back behind the wheel of a car gave him a sense of comfort that he hadn't expected. *I never thought I'd be able to endure driving on the highway again after…* He decided not to remind himself, lest it upset him. One thing he knew for sure: sitting in the passenger seat for so long had made him feel helpless. Despite the fact that it wasn't his car, he knew that he felt better being in control.

Once Calleigh had settled into the passenger seat and they were out on the road, she fell asleep. The dog whined from the back seat and cocked his head as she faded out.

"Guess it's just you and me, Ton," Spencer said under his breath, staring into the rearview mirror.

The corgi lay down on the seat and stared up at him, his large brown eyes filled with confusion.

It wasn't until dark that they crossed into New York State. The scenery didn't change all at once like Spencer had expected it would. Instead, the cities gradually gave way to wide fields of green grass and barns with weathered wood that stuck out against the glare of the headlights. Even the smell was different. The never-ending scent of exhaust and dog urine seemed to vanish all together and was replaced by a crisp bite of summer in the country. The smells of hay carried on the wind that rolled down the hills off on their right.

Spencer lost himself to seamless, unspooling thoughts about his ex-wife, work, and what he'd be doing if he were at home right then. Would he have been beating himself up for not going with Calleigh? Or would he have already forgotten all about it? Would he be onto something else in his life to complain about?

"Aren't you getting tired?" Calleigh asked suddenly, jarring him out of his recollections.

He checked the clock on the dash. "It's only nine."

She looked at him for a moment until he glanced back at her. "You've been driving for nearly five hours straight. Don't you think we should take a break, maybe find a place to hole up for the night?"

He glanced out his window. "Calleigh, I don't know if you've noticed but we seem to be somewhere between Mayberry and Old MacDonald's farm. We're not going to find a hotel all the way out—"

Calleigh pointed at something up ahead on his side. "What's that?"

He squinted. A Victorian styled house sat at the top of the hill they were climbing, a little light burning brightly at the end of the driveway. Beside it was a sign that was barely readable in the night. Below a smaller sign rocked in the breeze, much easier to read: vacancy.

Calliegh leaned back in her seat, smiling. "What were you were saying, Spence?"

"There isn't even a gas station around here." He waved his arm. "We should keep driving until we find some place that looks like civilization."

She chuckled. "Come on. I need a break from this car, you need a break from this car…"

"I'm doing fine."

"Your hand is shaking."

His eyes flicked down to it. It was and not just slightly either. He gave it a couple of sharp wags.

Calleigh had continued talking, not even noticing. "…probably have some kind of caffeine deficiency, for all I know."

"All right, we'll stop for the night," he gave in. He pulled the car off the road into the inn's driveway and killed the engine.

Calleigh snagged the keys from him as she climbed out. "I'll bet you're dehydrated. I haven't seen you take one sip of water in the last five hours."

"God, what the hell are you? Some kind of Nazi nutritionist? I drink water."

She popped the trunk. "When was the last time?"

"That rest stop in Massachusetts."

"That was *hours* ago. You're not a camel! It probably took thirty minutes for you to sweat it all out in today's heat."

"Hey, I didn't pull over so you could lecture me."

She unexpectedly tossed her bag at him, which he caught only just barely. "You're right. I'll take the dog for a walk. You get us a room." With that, she rounded the car to the backseat and pulled the dog out. She marched up the hill with Newton eagerly leading the way before Spencer could protest.

Grabbing his own backpack out of the trunk, he slung it over his shoulder and started up the front walk. The place had a grandmotherly appeal to it, a white picket fence separating the front yard from the parking lot, bushes on either side of the door painstakingly clipped to perfection. He climbed the steps to the front porch and twisted the ornate knob on the mahogany door.

Inside, a waft of potpourri tackled his nose much like lion would a tired antelope. Momentarily taken aback, he gazed around the front room of the inn and cringed. There were doilies everywhere. They hung ornamentally from the rungs of the staircase in front of him, placed under decorative candles and centerpieces on the tables

40

left and right. Even the rug beneath him resembled a giant doily. And even stranger, there were bowls of water all over the place, just sitting in random corners of the house.

"Can I help you, young man?" someone called to him from the next room over. He saw a desk there, although no one seemed to be behind it. As he got closer, he noticed a patch of hair just barely sticking up over the edge of the countertop. Once he'd stopped at the desk, he could see her fully, an old lady standing barely four feet tall, straightening papers beneath the counter. She looked up at him with the strangest clear blue eyes and said, "May I help you?"

"Yeah, I'd like to, uh, rent a room?"

She frowned.

He did the same. "Just for the night?"

The old woman came out from behind the counter and stared at the ground next to Spencer. "Rent a room for who?"

Spencer looked around himself. "For myself and a friend."

She crooked her finger and beckoned him closer. He knelt toward her. And then she said in the sweetest way, "There's nobody with you, hon."

"She's out taking the dog for a walk."

"Oh, so you do have an animal."

Spencer's shoulders dropped as he suddenly paid more attention to the surroundings. Crocheted mats with shapes of dogs hung on different places on the walls. Not only were there bowls of water but bowls of kibble placed strategically around the house, each

41

with a little doily under it.

He looked back at the old lady. "Excuse me for a moment."

*

Once he'd returned to the spot near the car, he quickly looked left and right before dropping the bags and shouting, "Calleigh!"

Her head popped out from the other side of the car. "I'm right here. What do you want?"

"The nice lady inside asked us if Newton would like a room with a television?"

She shook her head. "What?"

"It's a doggy hotel!"

She rounded him and looked at the sign. Carved into the wood and set in silver leaf were the words "Creature Comforts" with a little terrier painted beneath. "So we can't get a room?"

"It all depends. Would you like a king or queen-sized doggy bed?"

"Well, maybe she'll let us sleep on the floor of one of the rooms…"

"Sure!" Spencer exclaimed. "And then, in the morning, we can have bones and kibble with the other guests, all served on lace doilies."

Calleigh shot him a glare. "It wouldn't hurt to ask."

"Forget it. I'll spend the night in the car." Spencer patted the roof of the Nissan.

"You wouldn't make it one hour, not with the backseat

smelling like dog pee."

He cringed. She was right. She'd spent the better part of twenty minutes trying to clean the floor mat at a rest stop earlier but could only do so much with the rain.

"We should ask where the nearest bed and breakfast is and go there." She marched up the walk to the house.

"That's great," he called. "I'll just wait out here." He shoved his hands into his pockets and leaned back against the car. Newton poked his head out the window next to him, panting happily while his tongue lolled.

Spencer squinted at him. "You don't strike me as a doily kind of dog."

A few minutes later, Calleigh came up the front walk, practically skipping. "Good news!"

"What?"

"There's a bed and breakfast just a few miles north of us. The lady inside drew me a map." She handed it to Spencer.

He blinked. "These are the directions?"

Calleigh nodded.

"You sure she wasn't just doodling?"

Calleigh growled, "Let's go." They climbed into the car and pulled out.

They followed the directions on the map, though it was more Calleigh going from memory than Spencer reading. He could barely make out the writing on this supposed "map". "Turn right at the…Furby?"

Calleigh shook her head. "I'm pretty sure that says "curve", but what do I know? Maybe New York is littered with Furbies."

They arrived outside a very large farm house with black shutters and a stone front walk. Inside, a younger woman was straightening up some clutter on the desk when they walked in. However, instead of a warm welcome, her eyes locked on Newton, waddling along at Calleigh's heels.

Oh, here it comes, Spencer realized.

"Sorry, folks. We don't allow dogs."

Spencer glanced at Calleigh and found her looking back at him with mutual disbelief.

"There's a doggy inn a few miles south of here," the lady continued with a somewhat forced smile. "I'm sure they must have a vacancy."

Chapter 4

The night burned off into a pale yellow morning. The clouds were still blue behind the black silhouette of the Allegheny Plateau. Golden light slowly swept down across the green valleys and rolling hills all around them. Calleigh pulled the car off the highway into a dirt parking lot and killed the engine. They'd left the inn earlier that morning after picking Newton up from the doily house and had been driving for nearly three hours. They'd just crossed over into Pennsylvania, heading toward the Ohio border.

For several moments, she and Spencer both just sat there in an early morning daze, too tired to continue driving but too hungry to sleep. Even Newton was quiet, sitting perked up in the back seat staring at the two of them. It wasn't until Spencer climbed out of the car that he took a good look at the building they'd stopped near.

The trailer looked as though it had been cut in half. An old neon sign glared through a dirty window: Patty's Diner. Spencer ran his eyes down the line of other cars in the lot. They seemed to get older and older, as if he was going back in time. A mid 90's Toyota Corolla was parked closest to them, then, a late 80's Pontiac, an early 60's Volkswagen Beetle…a John Deere tractor. He stopped, just knowing the next was likely to be a horse and buggy.

Calleigh opened her door and climbed out, stretching her hands up to the sky as she groaned.

"You can't be serious about this place," he murmured.

"I thought you said you were hungry."

"I did. So why did we stop *here*?" He looked at the highway. "Why not stop at the next rest stop with at least reliably edible food."

"I support small businesses," Calleigh said.

"There's a difference between small and microscopic."

"What is your problem now?"

Spencer circled around the car to her. "I've been to places like this before. Places where you wonder if they pay the taxidermist to deliver his latest scrapings from the highway."

"Are you this big of a jerk about everything?"

"Just watch. Soon enough it will be "Eggs over-easy. Would you like a side of possum with that?""

Newton whined from the car.

Calleigh rolled her eyes and went for the door. "Come on. Let's get the road kill while it's still fresh, shall we?" She glanced back at Newton. "Be a good boy. We'll be right back." She opened the diner door and a cloud of hot smoky air rolled out. Both of them coughed as they carefully entered.

Patty's Diner was barely big enough to fit the bar counter and a few tiny tables with plastic blue checkered cloths. Everyone huddled around the tables or perched over the counter was over two hundred pounds. It required some squeezing and stomach sucking to get to a table over in the corner. The moment Spencer sat down, claustrophobia smothered him like a blanket.

A fuzzy song by Johnny Cash and June Carter Cash hummed over the tinny speaker in the corner of the ceiling, just barely enough for him to hear it. Forks scraped against plates, coffee slurped through patrons' lips, and grumbles of conversation buzzed all around them.

Spencer picked up the plastic covered menu on the table and instantaneously dropped it. Streaks of oily fingerprints covered it. He noticed Calleigh leave hers on the table and casually flip it with her fingertips when she came to the end.

"Welcome to Patty's Diner, gorgeous."

The voice startled him. It was the voice of a bulky hot dog vendor from the city who'd sucked on cigarettes for an entire life. It should have come from someone manly and gigantic. But when he glanced over his shoulder, he found a petite woman with more wrinkles than a bed sheet and bags beneath her heavily done-up eyes. Mascara-coated, spider leg eyelashes seemed to reach out toward him and he subconsciously leaned away.

"Good morning," Calleigh answered. She didn't even look phased.

"My name's Patty. I'll be your server today," the woman said with little emotion.

"The Patty that owns this place?" Spencer asked, somehow gaining his voice back.

"Owner and sole server." She put a finger to her lips for a

moment. "I guess 'sole' in both senses of the word. I serve people's souls, too."

Calleigh beamed like a Christmas tree in July. "It's a pleasure to meet you."

"Can I start you both off with a cup of joe?"

"That would be great."

Patty's eyes flicked to Spencer and the spider's legs twitched slightly.

"Coffee's good. Th-thanks," he sputtered.

"Coming up in two seconds, doll." She was off on her two spindly legs, weaving expertly between tables and was back behind the counter in a jiffy.

"She seems to like you, Spence," Calleigh commented, not looking up from her menu.

"Stupendous."

"Maybe once we eat, your mood will have changed."

"I'd feel better if you didn't keep playing Debbie Washington over there."

"Debbie Washington?"

He leaned back in his chair. "Debbie was a disturbingly optimistic girl that I went to high school with. Huge teacher's pet, pretty sure she had zero friends… *Macbeth* made her bawl for an hour in our sophomore English class."

"So, she was sensitive. Give her a break."

"I swear she did it to aggravate the rest of us. She'd bring the teachers an apple every day. She told us it was her parents who made her bring them but I'd started to wonder if she'd cornered the market."

"She sounds like she was a nice girl." Calleigh scoffed. "You should try it sometime."

"What? Being a nice girl?"

She tried to stare him down but a touch of a smile lit on her lips. "You know what I meant."

"Do I have to wear that sickly sweet smile of her's, too?" Spencer smiled so hard that his head began to hurt.

Calleigh's eyes went wide. "Don't ever do that again."

"Told you it was scary."

A cup of coffee plunked down in front of him, some sploshing up over the sides and onto the paper placemat. Patty had once again silently sidled up to him.

"Cream and sugar is on the table," she hoarsely informed them, leaning over Spencer's shoulder to put Calleigh's coffee down. The smell of bacon grease and an old sponge made his vision nearly mist over. Over the speakers, a song suspiciously like "Dueling Banjos" began to play.

"Have you decided what you'd like for breakfast?" Patty whipped an order pad out of her apron almost as fast as a cowboy's quick draw.

"Do you have any specials today?" Calleigh asked.

"It's special if Ralph can get it out of the pan before it burns." Patty's expression was deadpan. After a moment, an enormous, "HA!"

escaped her lipstick-caked mouth followed by what was either laughing or her lungs collapsing.

Calleigh chuckled oddly.

"I'm just teasing you," she said. "We've got a trout omelet for the special."

Trout? Spencer thought. *Is there even a lake nearby?*

Calleigh coughed. "I'll stick with some scrambled eggs."

"Any sides with that?"

"Bacon."

"Sorry, Ralph wasn't able to take care of Philly today. So, no bacon or sausage today."

"Philly?" Spencer croaked.

"He's one of our pigs: Philly, Milly, Jilly, and Spot."

"Ah." Calleigh nodded. "Just some toast then. Wheat."

Patty jotted it down and spun toward Spencer. "And for you, hon?" The banjo-plucking quickened in the background.

"Blueberry pancakes."

"Fantastic," she murmured as she wrote it down. "Just made the batter for that this morning."

"Lucky me."

The silverware jumped as Calleigh's shoe slammed into his shin under the table. He stifled a groan as she tossed him a glare to accompany it.

"Anything to go along with that?" Patty asked, totally oblivious.

"What's the 'Brown Sugar Walnut Syrup'?"

"That's my great-granddaddy's recipe. I've been making it for nearly forty years. You'll love it."

"Okay."

"Be back in a little bit." And she was off.

He leaned over the table toward Calleigh. "As long as it's not the same batch from forty years ago, I'm sure it will be great."

Calleigh had a far off expression. "The poor pigs…"

"I'm sure they've got piglets Larry, Garry, and Barry fattening up for later," he said, taking a sip of his coffee. It was like pouring hot oil down his throat. It bubbled and sizzled as it hit his empty stomach. He put the mug back down and stared at the mini tar pit in it, half expecting to see a fossil surface.

Calleigh watched him. "Any good?"

He shook his head. "Trust me. You'll *want* this one light and sweet."

She snatched two packets of sugar, ripped them open and poured them in. Next, a little plastic pocket of cream joined them. She went for her spoon.

Spencer stared at her a moment, then flicked his gaze back to the cream. "Add another. Trust me."

She did so and then stirred. Just as she had raised the mug to her lips, there was a blast of coughing from a table behind them.

An older man sitting at a table a few feet from them was convulsing in his chair as though he'd been electrocuted. His hands were at his throat, his tongue protruding from between his lips as he gasped to breathe.

Calleigh's chair scraped the floor and she rushed over to him. Her arms wrapped around the man's chest as she urged him into a standing position. She clasped her hands together and pulled them in and up into him.

Spencer had seen the Heimlich in action several times before. He'd even been taught to do it unsuccessfully in summer camp when he was a kid before others had to take over for him. But now as with all those other times, he was transfixed by the scene in front of him as if it wasn't real somehow.

Calleigh pulled up again on her arms. This time, the man's mouth opened and with his cough, something launched through the diner air like a shuttle heading for space. Calleigh let him slump into his chair.

After a few more hacks, the man turned and clasped her hands in his large calloused ones. "Thank you, dear," he said breathlessly, his face reddened.

Calleigh gave him a close-lipped smile, slipped her hand out from his, and said, "It's no problem."

Spencer frowned.

The man chuckled awkwardly and said, "Well, I might have died if you hadn't been here."

She didn't say anything as she gazed around the diner. The rest of the patrons stared back at her, a sense of admiration glowing in their faces.

Spencer wasn't sure if she recognized her new celebrity status though. She seemed shut off somehow like she didn't want any part of it.

"What's your name, dear?" he asked her.

Spencer waited for her to give it…and waited…and waited.

She just patted the man on the shoulder. "You're welcome." Then, before he or anyone else could say anything more, she slunk back to her seat. When she sat down across from Spencer, she avoided eye contact and slurped from her coffee. Within a few more minutes, the buzz of conversation had returned.

""It's no problem?"" Spencer repeated, trying to catch her eyes. "What the hell kind of an answer is that? You just saved that guy's life!"

"Someone else would have stepped up if I hadn't."

"With this crowd? I kind of doubt it, unless Patty's soul-serving means she's a part-time paramedic."

She just stared out the window toward the parking lot. The sun bleached her face, and the blue checkered plastic on the table reflected on her chin. She wasn't going to talk anymore about it.

Spencer snagged a sugar packet from the bowl on the table and tore at it slowly. Though he really wanted to get to the bottom of her clumsy humbleness, he refrained. "So, what's the itinerary today?"

That familiar brightness filled her eyes as she leaned toward him, elbows on the table. "I thought maybe we'd try for Illinois."

"Three states away? I think we can manage that."

"Well, who knows what we'll run into on our way: summer traffic, congested cities, accidents… We'll be passing pretty close to Toledo and pretty much straight through Cleveland. We may not even make it to Chicago."

The thought of being caught in yet another city's traffic ushered a groan from him. He knew it would have to happen, but his patience for it was worn thin by what he knew Newton's reaction would be. The dog would get panicky, flop over the divide between the front and back seat, scramble up over his lap and Calleigh's in order to poke his fat head out the windows. Spencer knew he couldn't deal with that for an hour's time. And if it rained? God forbid they'd have to deal with an episode like the one yesterday.

"What if we took a different route? Maybe take route 69 down to 70? We could avoid Chicago that way."

"But we'd hit all the other big cities. Indianapolis, St. Louis and Kansas City."

Spencer's lip turned up. "Ick."

"Plus, it would take more time to get to Oregon," Calleigh said, "which probably wouldn't be a good idea, seeing as how your boss only gave you the two weeks leave."

He sighed. Oh, that's right. He still had a life to get back to when this crazy trip was over. It wasn't enough that he wasn't even taking a vacation to a place he actually wanted to go. It was that after he'd endured the entire exhausting car trip, he'd have to saunter back into the courtroom with his head hanging and keep doing that job.

As Calleigh dug into her pack beneath the table, his mind wandered to the apartment he'd left back in Maine. He thought about the bare walls, how Lydia's paintings used to hang on them. He hadn't bothered to put anything back up after she'd gone. He just didn't see the point. Why cover up what was there? Everything seemed blank anyway.

His nose alerted him that Patty had returned with their food. Along with her old sponge smell, there was an intoxicating maple aroma that infected his senses. When she set the plate down in front of him, he suddenly remembered how hungry he was. Two blueberry-speckled pancakes gazed up at him from the plate. Their butter-coated surfaces gleamed, the shine of maple syrup like liquid bronze trickling over their hills and valleys. There in that greasy little diner out in the middle of nowhere, those pancakes looked like the most beautiful things he'd ever laid eyes on.

Patty set Calleigh's eggs down and stood back, hands on her hips. "Now, you tell me how you like that syrup, okay, darling?"

Spencer hadn't even noticed her term of endearment. He just thanked her and took up his fork and knife. Slicing free a small square, he popped it in his mouth, a small part of him expecting the worst.

Words couldn't describe it. It was as though he was ten again and anxiously anticipating his mom's pancakes before school. He closed his eyes and allowed himself to be lost inside the memory.

When he opened them again, he noticed Calleigh smiling at

him from across the table.

"What?"

"Nothing. You just looked like you…got a boner or something."

"What can I say? I guess great grand-daddy added mojo to his syrup."

"That good, huh?"

"It's unbelievable," he said, taking another bite. He diced another piece with the fork, and held it across the table to her. "You're going to have a mini orgasm. Believe me."

She took it from him hesitantly and slid it off the fork with her teeth. Her eyes rounded instantly. "Whoa."

He took the fork back and dug back into his pancakes. Calleigh bit into a piece of toast. "Try finding that at one of your fast-food places," she added.

Spencer stopped eating and glanced over his shoulder. Patty was welcoming an older couple into the restaurant with hugs and handshakes. She sat them down at a table near the window and poured them coffee, all the while, her hoarse voice combed the air amidst the random blurbs of conversation.

A soul server… The words came back to him as he turned back to his pancakes.

Chapter 5

Crossing into Ohio hadn't changed the scenery much. The forests and green farmlands of Pennsylvania had quietly converted to similarly lush fields with tall grass. Corn stretched back into a sea of stalks that coated the hills for what seemed like miles. Spencer, behind the wheel once again, let his sunglasses slide down the bridge of his nose in order to take in the full spectrum of colors from a plant nursery on the roadside. Purples, oranges, and yellows blushed in patches from the various tables out front.

The colors in the flowers seemed fake somehow, shades too vibrant for the green of the countryside. They transported him somewhere infinitely warmer, somewhere with a crisp sea air that tasted of salt with the littlest hint of fish. Bright whites, capped by rich blues and accented with freckles of red and salmon pink, and coal black cliffs edging the frothy azure sea.

Lydia's hair was long then. Pulled into a fishtailed braid, it swung behind her as she ran toward the marketplace. Her skin was still white from spending so much time inside back home. But her pale complexion fit her and made her seem that much more flawless. He could still see his hands sliding up her thighs the night before in the hotel room, counting the few freckles he found. As she ran, she laughed about something. The sound was lost in the wind. He couldn't remember her laugh very well, he realized.

He'd been chasing her, trying to lure her back to their room for an afternoon of relaxation and possibly more thigh caressing. "Catch me if you can, Sparky," she'd called before taking off. He wasn't going to let her get away.

Rustle.

He glanced over at Calleigh. She was trying to refold the map of Ohio, but was failing miserably. Finally, she made a bunch of new folds in it and tucked it down next to her seat.

"You know," he said, "I'm beginning to realize that you know way more about me than I know about you. It's kind of unfair."

"Unfair?"

"It's also a little creepy."

"Well, what do you want to know?"

"For starters, how about what you do for a living?"

"I teach."

He blew a raspberry. "Well, that's vague."

"You didn't ask for specifics."

"I think I implied specifics."

"I teach environmental sustainability."

"There! See that wasn't so hard, was it?"

She stared out her window.

"So, what about outside of work? What do you like to do for fun?"

She paused. "Torture unsuspecting people in coffee shops."

He chuckled. "Oh, I got that. But, seriously, what do you and your friends like to do?"

The smile dissipated from her face. She didn't say anything.

He frowned. "You don't want to tell me? That's fine. I was just trying to start a conversation."

She scoffed flippantly. "If it's fine, then don't keep asking me."

"Whoa, whoa, danger," he said. "I wasn't interrogating you."

Her cheeks reddened but no apology came. Instead, she just pulled the map back out and lost herself in it.

Spencer wasn't sure he wanted to ask her anything else personal for the rest of the day. She was obviously still stewing on what had transpired earlier at the diner.

It wasn't much later that they found the greens fading back into greys and were lost in the confines of the cities, with clusters of buildings rising high around them. Spencer once again found his thoughts withdrawn toward the honeymoon week in Greece, memories that seemed to have holes in them. Every time Lydia laughed in his mind's eye, there was no sound to accompany it.

They cleared the various exits and turn-offs through Cleveland, not making conversation other than Calleigh calling out directions. As they finally found themselves on the Ohio interstate, the traffic grew more congested. The little Nissan was soon boxed in by semi-trucks on three sides. Their airbrakes released almost in unison like bursts of steam from vents in the bottom of some rusty old tanker. The view wasn't much better. It pulled Calleigh out of her self-isolation in time to point a finger to this left. "Watch it!"

A truck was trying to change lanes to make room for a red convertible that was cruising up the fast lane. The driver hadn't even seen them.

Spencer tapped the brakes and yanked on the steering wheel. The car jerked into the next lane over, cutting off an advancing Honda, one of those cars that he'd always thought looked like a bread box. A chorus of honking filled the air. The big truck's shadow slid over them.

His view of the road was blocked from all sides. A familiar feeling crept into his gut, something uncomfortable that made goosebumps rise on his arms despite the temperature.

Newton barked suddenly and he jerked in his seat. "Jesus…" he said under this breath. The feeling spread through him like oil contaminating water.

On the other side of the semi next to them, he heard the red convertible gun its engine and zoom by.

"That asshole…" Calleigh muttered under her breath.

The car was getting warmer and warmer. Spencer crooked his finger into his shirt collar. It was soaked with sweat. His eyes flicked to the rearview mirror, searching for some kind of an exit.

The trucks were matching speeds on either side of him. The middle lane seemed to be gridlocked with the longest string of vehicles. His fingers slid on the steering wheel rubber when he shifted his hands and a bitter taste stung the tip of his tongue.

I have to get to that outside lane. I have to.

"Spence?"

Calleigh was cautiously giving him a once over. Her voice sounded like it was miles away.

He blinked. "I…uh…"

"Spencer?"

"I need some water."

Her fingers closed over his right hand. He was suddenly aware that it had been shaking.

"What's wrong?"

"I need to get off the highway." He took a breath but couldn't seem to get enough air. "Now."

Calleigh's thumb punched the emergency lights button on the dash. Her fist pounded on the horn and the sound swallowed up the low groans of the trucks on either side of them. In what seemed like seconds, light purged the area as the truck to their right slowed down and space opened up in front of it. Newton began yipping frantically.

"Okay…" Spencer wheezed.

Calleigh's grip didn't loosen over his on the steering wheel. The moment there was enough room, she flicked the blinker and yanked the steering wheel over into the slow lane. They stayed there for a time.

The feeling of claustrophobia slowly dissipated in his mind. The air became easier. He took a deep breath. There was a loud ringing in his ears. "It's okay. I'm okay."

Calleigh shook her head. "We're pulling off at the next rest stop."

"I'm not arguing with you there. But I can drive. It's okay."

"You're sure?"

"Yeah."

She reluctantly let go of his hand. It was still quivering. He took it off the wheel and laid it in his lap as if it were broken. They passed a green sign with the next exit two miles away.

"What the hell just happened to you?" Calleigh asked.

"I'll explain when we stop."

They took the next turn off and followed the curl of the road to the tollbooth. Spencer shoved a few dollars into the lady's hand and found the closest place to pull over; a gas station with petrol-streaked concrete.

He clicked the seatbelt and let it slither off him. Before Calleigh could ask any questions, he popped the door open and climbed out. His legs somehow carried him inside the gas station, not even pausing when Calleigh's door opened behind him and he heard her call his name.

Inside, he locked himself in the bathroom. Back up against the door, he slid down to a sitting position and dug into his pocket for his pills. He stared at them, eyes round with realization. It was a bad idea to have gone on this trip. It was a bad idea not to have told Calleigh. It was all bad.

Someone knocked on the door.

He stood and went to the sink. With a scoop of water in his palm, he took a pill and swallowed it. The knocking at the door continued.

"I'll be out in a minute," he called, splashing his face. He'd rather have stayed in that bathroom for the next hour rather than go out there and tell Calleigh. That wasn't an option though. *Someone's going to crap their pants if I don't eventually come out.*

He unlocked the door and pushed it open, allowing an antsy teen the chance to slip inside. He lingered in the convenience store for a moment, bought a package of powdered donuts and bottled water. When he pushed outside, he found Calleigh returning Newton to the car. When she noticed Spencer, she leaned up against the car, her expression carved by worry.

"You okay?"

"Yeah." He held up the donuts. "I got you these. I doubt they're still edible. They're hard as rocks and probably have been sitting on the shelf for ten years."

Her gaze didn't leave his face. "What happened to you?"

He sighed. Digging into his pocket, he found his pills and handed them to her.

She read the label. "Fluoxetine? An anti-depressant?"

"I get panic attacks."

His words hung in the air for a moment as Calleigh looked at him, her expression slowly becoming more confused.

"I thought you were having a heart attack," she finally said. "I was this close to calling an ambulance for you."

"It's a disorder. I don't have any control over when it happens." Inside, he felt deflated.

"You didn't think it was worth mentioning this disorder to me before we left Maine?" Calleigh's eyes were wide, like a hawk on the verge of swooping down on a mouse.

"I didn't."

"Why?"

"I haven't had an attack that bad in weeks."

Calleigh combed her hair with her fingers absentmindedly. A truck released its airbrakes at the stoplight nearby and he jumped in spite of himself.

Calleigh's look softened. "How long has this been a problem?"

"Five years."

She didn't say anything for a while. The sounds of traffic gnawed at the space between them. He hoped she wasn't thinking of more questions to ask. He still felt hot and nauseous. He would have much rather had an awkwardly silent car ride over the imminent interrogation.

She blinked once and tossed him his pill bottle. "Are you okay to get back in the car?"

He held his stomach. "I just need a little time not driving, enough for this to kick in." He shook the pills and returned them to his pocket.

She checked her watch. "It's almost one. It's my turn to take the wheel anyway. We'll get to the next rest stop, and snag some food there. Then maybe you can drive when we reach Indiana?"

He was expecting more unease from her, expecting her to freak out a little or imply that she would drive the rest of the time. But he was glad that she hadn't been predictable; hadn't been like Lydia. "I'll take the wheel for the evening shift."

"All right."

They climbed back in the car and Calleigh turned them around to get back to the highway. The tension in his shoulders was loosening up just as they merged with traffic on the interstate. Thankfully, there were no semi-trucks in sight.

Chapter 6

Less than ten minutes after they were back on the interstate, Spencer had slipped into a daze, staring at the blurring scenery out his window. He didn't remember falling asleep. When the car squeaked into a parking place at a rest stop, the blackness bloomed to pearls of light. The sky had an orange sherbet hue to it. The smell of gasoline and greasy food lifted the last of sleep's hold on him. He sat up and rubbed his face. When he looked over his shoulder, he noticed Newton's muzzle just inches away.

He scrunched up his nose. "Newton, your breath might as well be the Bubonic plague."

"Have a good nap?" Calleigh asked, before taking a swig of her water.

He nodded. "How long was I out?"

"About an hour or so. We just passed Toledo. Indiana's coming right up."

"Food?"

"Yeah." She chuckled. "You weren't kidding about those donuts being inedible earlier."

He noticed a crumpled wrapper in the cup holder. "I'm a master in the ways of weird and wonderful road snacks," he said.

They both got out of the car. Calleigh pulled the cooler from the trunk and opened a plastic container filled with raw meat cubes, a green puree that looked as though it had been ladled from a swamp, and a colorful variety of fruit slices. Spencer stared at it as she put a few zucchini slices in Newton's dog bowl.

"Did you stop and raid a farm while I was asleep?"

"We stopped at a market. You were dead to the world so I figured I'd let you sleep."

"They didn't sell any dog food at this store?"

"I don't buy into all of that canned dog food bullshit," Calleigh said, replacing the lid on the container and putting it back in the cooler. "I think the raw food diet is much healthier for Newton than all of that preserved crap."

Spencer raised his brows. "Don't hold back. Tell me how you really feel."

"Don't you ever wonder what's really in that stuff; the additives and by-products that aren't clearly identified on the labels?"

"Well, they have to have additives. The stuff sits on shelves in the grocery store. Sometimes, for years!"

"Like those donuts, right?"

Spencer shook his head. "So, when a pet food commercial is saying that it's got chicken, peas, and carrots in it, you don't believe them for a moment?"

"I think they want you to believe there's a chicken pot pie in the dog food and it's going to make your dog faster, fitter, and stronger." She put the bowl in the car for Newton.

His wedge-shaped head dug into the food and his happy slurping cut Spencer off from his rebuttal. He wasn't the person to try and fight her on pet food of any kind, not when Daffodil the cat had died choking on a chicken bone.

Calleigh snagged her wallet from the car and shut the door. As Spencer walked around the car to join her, she froze.

"What?"

She stared intently across the parking lot and his gaze followed hers. There, parked across the lot away from most of the other vehicles, was the red convertible that had passed them earlier.

Calleigh's eyes were now set in a glare of supreme malice, a glare that vaguely reminded him of the squirrel-strangling gaze of Gina Sutton from the Donat Leroy Case back home. He put a hand tentatively on her shoulder. "Let it go."

"I love how he's strategically parked his car away from everyone else. He must be afraid of the paint getting scratched." She glanced down at her car keys jangling in her hand.

"Don't."

"Why not?"

"You're not some high-school bimbo getting revenge on your ex-boyfriend by scratching up his prized car."

"Did you go to a high school modeled after *Grease*?"

He crossed his arms. "I'm serious."

"The girls in my high school never keyed their ex-boyfriends' cars," she acknowledged. "They just slept with their ex's best friends."

"Well, I recommend you don't do that either."

"He needs a reminder that he shares the highway with other people—"

"He's a pretentious asshole, Calleigh; one pompous ass-hat in a sea of them. He's not worth it."

" —and contrary to his beliefs in the way of the pretentious asshole, he isn't King of the Road."

"Scratching up his car isn't going to make him stop driving like a jerk," Spencer said, putting a hand on Calleigh's shoulder and guiding her toward the building. "It'll just make him more pissed off and he'll drive even crazier. Then, something worse might happen."

Her feet stuck like stones and she slipped his hand off of her. For a few moments, he wondered if she'd gotten the wrong idea. He got his answer when she gave him a pat on his chest. "Go and get us some food. I'm going to leave the King of the Road a note."

There was no stopping her, he realized. Once Calleigh had something set in her mind, it was like trying to change the opinion of a political party. She was stuck on the idea that a little gesture like a note would actually make a difference. He scoffed and started inside. "Don't get caught!" he called back over his shoulder as he pushed inside the air-conditioned building.

The place was flooded with people. Various tables and chairs stood in the center of the circular room. All around were various fast-food amenities, each one packed with lines of hungry freeway travelers. The room carried a strangely sickening combination of a deep-fryer and air-freshener. It reminded him of a funeral parlor that had set up shop next to a Wendy's back in Maine. He'd overlooked it from his office across the road various times, wondering how difficult it would be to comfort grieving families while someone shouted "One Baconator with fries" through an intercom in the background.

He gazed around the room, a part of him wondering if he could pick out the owner of the red convertible by their appearance. There was a mix-mash of all types from motorcyclists in heavy leather wolfing down burgers, to a finicky business woman carefully sliding pickles off her sandwich with a face scrunched up tighter than a rejected love note. For a few minutes, he favored her as the driver but then noticed her Audi keys dangling from the pocket of her blazer. The car outside was a Chrysler.

His stomach was sour and a stale taste lingered in his mouth. Spencer quickly rejected any ideas of deep-fried goodies and turned into the store. There, he found a couple turkey and Swiss sandwiches and paired them up with a Coke and lemon-lime soda.

One of the many things Calleigh had yammered about the previous day while they were stuck in the traffic jam was that she despised dark sodas and absolutely couldn't stand grape soda.

"I've heard it kills men's sperm," she'd said after taking a long swig of water.

"If we used our penises as straws …" he'd muttered under his breath.

"Seriously. I heard it somewhere."

"Maybe from Fox news?"

She hadn't continued but instead stuck out her tongue at him, the revenge of a four year old girl to a little boy who's just called her a booger-head.

There was only one other person in the store; a woman standing on heels so vertical, they might as well have been stilts. Her cropped leggings made her calves bulge. The white tank top she wore was most definitely one or two sizes too small and accentuated all her sets of love handles. Her sunglasses looked identical to the ones worn by Gary Oldman in Coppola's *Dracula*. While Spencer stood trying to decide between corn and potato chips, she smacked her gum and took a pull from the beer mug full of what he hoped was apple juice.

"…mustard and hamburger buns!" she declared suddenly.

Only when she turned did Spencer notice the Bluetooth headset in her ear.

"Oh my god, Jonna, you didn't!"

Spencer quickly snapped up a jar of peanuts and turned for the counter. He passed the window looking out on the parking lot. Beyond lines of vehicles, he noticed Calleigh and Newton poised by the red convertible. Newton lifted one of his stubby legs as a stream of urine splashed on the flashy rims of the convertible's wheels.

Spencer's back stiffened as a terrible realization spread over him like a sickness. Count Stiltsula turned toward the counter, still hip-deep in conversation with "Jonna". Her keys jangled wildly in her left hand, sharing room with several packages of chocolate cookies.

Ironically in the other hand, he noticed a plastic container with a Caesar salad. But the Chrysler symbol on her keys couldn't have stood out any more than it did in those few seconds.

The woman stepped up to the counter, spilling all of her goodies.

"Well, I know that's what she *said*, Jonna, but that isn't what she *meant*…"

The cashier, a college-age girl, stared at her for a moment before she started scanning each chocolate cookie.

Spencer slipped his mobile out of his pocket and quickly dialed Calleigh. There was no way he could pay for his items and get outside in time to warn her. He glanced outside again, noticing Calleigh negotiate Newton to one of the other wheels to resume peeing.

Ring.

The woman slapped her credit card down on the counter, just barely missing the girl's hand as she picked up the last chocolate cookie. "Haven't you been listening to a word I've been saying?" she broadcast into the headset.

Ring.

Another couple that had walked into the store shot sympathetic gazes toward the girl behind the counter.

Ring.

Pick up, Calleigh. Pick up.

"Your total is seventeen dollars and thirty four cents," the girl said.

The woman picked up her card and shoved it practically in the girl's face. "Can't you see I'm talking to someone?" she proclaimed with effrontery. "Yes, I'm still here, Jonna."

The couple, now to Spencer's right, exchanged glances. From where they stood, they couldn't see the woman's Bluetooth. They probably figured she had an acute case of schizophrenia.

Finally, the phone picked up. "Hey, where are you?" Calleigh asked. Wind blew into the speaker and muffled her voice slightly.

"Stop what you're doing right now," he commanded, trying to keep his voice down.

She looked around wildly. "Where are you?"

"I'm in the convenience store, and the convertible driver is in here, too."

He glanced behind him. The woman was muttering over her phone as she scribbled a loop-de-loop signature onto the receipt that the cashier timidly slid over to her.

"Did they see me?"

"I doubt it. She's too busy giving the cashier hell. But she's on her way out."

She scoffed. "Well, then I'm glad I let Newton do his thing. She sounds like a real winner."

The woman snatched her receipt from the cashier and cast a look at Spencer that made the air suddenly seem thin. "I'll be sure to mention that to her," he said, shooting an uneasy smile in the woman's direction. Once she was out of earshot, he added, "I'm sure Jonna will be thrilled to hear the news."

"Who?"

"Nothing. I'll see you at the car."

He slapped the phone shut and brought the sandwiches and soda to the counter.

The girl was visibly shaken as she scanned his items, not once making eye contact. Apparently, she hadn't had this job long. He imagined anyone who worked at a rest stop and saw hundreds of different people each day would have developed a tough skin to bizarre and rude behavior.

"Two dollars and fifteen cents is your change."

"Thank—"

"Excuse me!"

He looked to his left. Stiltsula had returned; Bluetooth now disengaged from her ear. For a moment, he wondered if she had discovered her car, if she'd overheard him on the phone. But her fury was once again directed toward the cashier. She was headed right for the place he was standing. He sidestepped her, just barely getting out of her way as she fished her receipt from the cookie bag and forked it over to the cashier. "You overcharged my card!"

From where he stood, he saw the error. It was an easy one to make; a seven had been replaced with a nine. But it didn't seem as though the cashier was going to get any sympathy from Vlad the Cookie Inhaler.

"I want this transaction voided. Now!"

"Lady," he spoke up, vaguely aware that he was endangering himself by getting involved, "Calm down. She made a mistake. Go easy on her."

She turned like cotton candy being spun slowly over a stick. The crystalline granules of shock melted into high, thick, and wispy pomposity. "This has nothing to do with you," she answered, her chest puffing up, "so I suggest you mind your own business."

Spencer could have argued. He felt the words leaping right up to his tongue, dozens of them just waiting to sling at her, vast vats of muddied insults that would have left her speechless, or would have at least diverted her cruel attacks on that cashier. But in the end, he shoved them down deep. She was right to a degree. And getting into a shouting match with her in the middle of a convenience store in Ohio wasn't quite what he'd planned for his afternoon itinerary.

He found himself nodding and grabbing his bag from the counter as he made his exit. He felt the desperate gaze of the cashier like ice on his back but fought the urge to turn around. Once outside, the sun burned the icy spots. The light felt suddenly pale and strange. By the time he'd reached Calleigh's car, he hadn't realized that he was gritting his teeth.

Calleigh peered out of the driver's window at him. "Who's Jonna?"

The scene in the convenience store replayed itself over and over in his head. He'd hoped that the girl had gotten hold of a manager or that someone else had spoken up to tell the lady to shut her mouth.

Then there was that sting of cowardice that threaded through him so tightly, he began to think that leaving hadn't been the right choice at all. People like that didn't listen to just one person. They were used to a pattern; they were manipulative to a degree and had mastered the various techniques of how to properly use it on poor unsuspecting people. A little urine on her car tires wasn't going to do a thing.

"Have you got a notepad or something in there that I can use?"

Calleigh reached over and popped the glove box open. She handed a small pad of paper to him. "You're going to leave her a note, aren't you?" she asked.

He ignored her as he slid a pen from his shirt pocket out, bit the cap off, and started scribbling. Though various vicious comments leapt to mind, he reined in his outrage enough to form a message that even she would understand and hopefully listen to.

"What'd you say?" Calleigh asked when he'd finished.

He capped the pen and slid it back into his pocket. "It says, "Your display in the convenience store was not only offensive but also ethically wrong. Next time you act like that—"

Calleigh leaned out the window, swiped the paper from his hand, and tore it up.

"Hey! What the…"

"You sound like a lawyer."

"Brilliant observation."

"With a touch of well-meaning grandma." She tossed the shredded pieces into the backseat of the car. Newton tried to eat the confetti as it fell. "It sounds like your charging her with indecent exposure in a public place."

"There could be an argument for that, too."

She took the notepad from him, found a pencil among the clutter of the glove box, and jotted down something quick. She handed it to him.

""'Karma's a bitch. Enjoy washing your tires.'""

"Simple, effective, and straight to the point," Calleigh said.

Newton gave an approving bark from the back.

"Fine." He glanced around to make sure the woman wasn't coming. Then, he quickly ran over to the car and deposited it beneath a wiper on the windshield. As he returned to the Nissan, he realized that Calleigh was right. There was no point in being effusive with this lady and writing her a mature note when her behavior had been childish. *Let her get angry about it.*

He got back to the car. "I'm driving right?"

"I'll stay behind the wheel a bit longer. We'll switch in a couple more hours."

He climbed into the passenger seat and buckled his seatbelt. "Let's go."

As Calleigh started the engine and backed out of the space, Spencer's eyes caught on the woman as she exited the front entrance of the rest stop. She was either muttering to herself in rage over the overcharging issue or was back on the line with Jonna and was telling her all about her latest drama. He watched her with a razor's edge of satisfaction, craning his head around to glimpse her as they drove by. She clop, clopped in her heels toward the parking lot, and veered toward the red convertible.

"Slow down," he told Calleigh, "I want to see her reaction."

The Nissan practically came to a stop in the lane as Calleigh, too, turned her attention to the convertible.

Except that the woman didn't go to the red car. She stopped short at a light sparkling blue sedan, oddly enough the color of sweet cotton candy, and unlocked it. Spencer looked on in horror as she tossed the bag of chocolate cookies and salad inside and slumped into the driver's seat.

Spencer spun toward Calleigh. "Drive."

Calleigh shrugged as she pressed the gas pedal. "The convertible driver still deserves what he got for the interstate stuff." Her tone didn't seem as sure about what they'd done as it had before.

"How does this affect *our* karma?" he asked out loud. Calleigh didn't answer.

Chapter 7

Calleigh took them across the border into Indiana. The sun was blinding as it began its descent behind the trees on the horizon. Spencer had switched places with her after they'd pulled off the interstate to let Newton out for a walk. While the scenery between Ohio and Indiana hadn't changed noticeably, Spencer was comforted with the idea that they were making headway. They still had several days of traveling and many more miles to deal with one another. He hadn't been sure about Calleigh at first. But with their camaraderie against the red convertible, he found his thoughts turning. *She's really not so bad.*

He drove until the sun had slipped below the black trees. The deep bloody orange sky cooled into a dusky purple that brought desires of sleep to the forefront of Spencer's mind. His legs cramped from hours of inactivity and his stomach still hadn't fully recovered from the episode with the semi-trucks earlier.

The wind rushed against his hair as he took a deep breath and said, "I'm going to sleep like a rock tonight."

"I'm right there with you," Calleigh answered, putting a hand up to adjust the black bandana on her head. She rolled down the sleeves on her red and blue plaid shirt and peered into the back seat at

Newton.

Spencer followed her gaze through the rearview mirror. The Corgi was sacked out on the seat on his back, legs curled up, and nose pointed straight up toward the sky. Every once in a while, he'd kick at the air and grunt.

Spencer chuckled. "Nice."

"My dog," Calleigh said with a smile. "Never has a problem getting to sleep."

"I envy him."

They eventually pulled off the interstate, heading south into a small farming community. Spencer's eyes read the name of the town and forgot it soon after. He was surprised he could even tell left from right at this point. The clock rounded on eight-thirty by the time they pulled up into a motor inn. Spencer stayed in the car with Newton while Calleigh went in to get them a room. He leaned the seat back and stared at the stained headliner, sighing. He heard a squeaky yawn from the back seat as Newton awoke and got up on his stubby legs. Seconds later, his head nuzzled up beside Spencer's on the headrest. He reached over his shoulder and hesitantly rubbed the Corgi's large ears.

"Did you two want some time alone?" Calleigh said from outside.

He looked up. "We got a room?"

"Down at the other end of the inn."

They negotiated the car down to the far end, collected their bags, and climbed the stairs to the top level. It was a cheaply designed room. There weren't even any gaudy paintings hung on the walls that were so common in these kinds of places. Two beds poked out on either side of a dark wooden nightstand with an alarm clock and a rotary phone.

"This brings back memories," Spencer said as he dropped his backpack on the bed and picked up the phone.

"My dad had one of those for a long time in his shop," Calleigh noted, slumping onto the bed closest to the door. Newton hopped up beside her, panting with excitement.

"What kind of shop?"

"Wood-working. He made furniture."

"I'm surprised."

"Why?" Calleigh glanced up at him quizzically.

"Well, the environmental conference, you being a granola and all…"

"How many times do I have to tell you I'm not a granola?"

He slumped onto the bed and unzipped his backpack. "Until you can make me believe otherwise."

She raised her eyebrows as she sat up. Reaching down to grab her pant leg, she suddenly yanked it up, rolling the jean up past her knee. "There."

Spencer stared. "What's that supposed to prove?"

"That I'm not a granola."

He cocked his head, as he put his backpack aside. "Your leg?"

"Well, I shave."

"I can see that."

Newton came around and laid his head in Calleigh's lap. "My point is that granolas usually aren't so hygienic…or at least they aren't according to your everyday average description of us 'flower children'."

"Listen, I didn't say you were Sasquatch and never in my assumption of granolas did I ever assume they didn't shave." He resumed looking in his bag until he came up with his toothbrush and toothpaste. "That's a nice leg, by the way."

She scowled and rolled her pant leg back down. "Then what's your definition, seeing as how you know me so well that you think you can judge me?"

Spencer got up and went into the bathroom. *Damn it. I've asked for it now.*

"Well?"

"Free-spirited…"

"I'll give you that one. What else?"

He ran the toothbrush under some water and squeezed the green gel onto it. "You like plants."

"I also like lasagna, beer, and a nice tan," she called. He could tell she was getting bored.

"You called my Lexus a gas-guzzler," he said, pushing the toothbrush in his mouth and scrubbing.

"Because it is!"

He scrubbed his teeth, desperately trying to come up with something else.

"Is that it? Is that the best you've got?"

He spit into the sink. "Not using the air-conditioning in the car."

"As I remember it, you had the opportunity to use it and you refused."

"The vent smelled like wet Newton."

The dog yapped from the other room.

"It's true."

Calleigh chuckled. "Honestly, Spence, if this is all you've got, I'm a bit disappointed."

He rinsed his mouth and spit again. As he went to the bathroom door, he noticed she was lying back on the bed once more, feigning interest in one of those year old magazines about house interiors that they keep in the rooms.

"The PTA shower."

The magazine slid down to reveal her furrowed brows. "The Parent Teacher Association?"

"Excuse me for sounding crude when I explain this but the pits, tits, and ass shower. It's the shower that people who don't want to waste a ton of water use, the type of shower that granolas use."

She shot up from the bed, eyes wide. "Have you been watching me shower?"

He grabbed the nearest thing, a towel, to defend himself. "No! I just noticed that you were only in the bathroom for a couple minutes tops this morning!"

Calleigh pointed a finger at him. He had the feeling that if she'd been blessed with telekinetic powers, she'd have thrown him into the mirror with just a flick of her wrist.

"Also," he added, "I hate to say it but you just confirmed it."

She opened her mouth but no sound came out. She closed it, a defiant grimace on her lips as she turned, went to the door, and opened it wide.

"Where are you going?"

She turned. "If I don't get away from you for a few minutes, Spencer, I just might have to kill you." She stormed out.

"Okay then," he said after she was well gone.

Newton glanced up at him from the bed and gave a shrill little bark.

"Remind me never to discuss showering habits with women I don't know," he said to the dog, sliding the towel back into the rack.

The corgi laid his nose down on his paws and groaned.

*

Calleigh returned from her walk about a half an hour later. The apples of her cheeks were reddened, though he couldn't be sure if it was from anger or the evening chill that had settled. Within moments of her coming back, her eyes lit up. "What's that smell?"

He slid a full plastic bag forward on the table, the characteristic yellow smiley face portending oily, gooey Asian delicacies within.

"Chinese food. There was a little place up the road. I took a stroll up there with Newton to pick it up."

"Wait. You *took* Newton?"

"He was itching to go for a walk. You hadn't taken him and I figured you wouldn't want to when you got back." He stood up and went over to the corgi who was lying in a chair on the opposite side of the room. "Granted, once we got there, they asked me how much I wanted to sell him for…"

Calleigh's eyes bulged.

"Kidding! I'm kidding."

She sat on the end of her bed and began picking at the tied-together handles on the plastic bag. "Well, I appreciate the gesture. Although, I'm not sure it quite makes up for your comment earlier."

Spencer lifted a box from behind the chair Newton rested in. "I also picked up some IPA."

Calleigh's smile returned. "You sure know your way out of the dog house, don't you?"

He pulled a bottle out and handed it to her. "My mouth has put me there many times before."

Popping the tops, they clinked the necks of their bottles together and dug into a buffet of crispy crab rangoon, juicy beef teriyaki on a skewer, red marinated chicken wings, and thick egg rolls. As Spencer bit into a crispy curl of fried shrimp, he thought back on the many long nights in law school that he'd stay awake into the bitter morning hours, where the only comfort and solace besides the promise of bed had been Chinese cuisine. It had been a saving grace of his for years until he and Lydia had moved in together. There were home cooked meals then, something that one or the other of them had worked hard to create. There wasn't the same ease and comfort that there had been in his youth. There wasn't that same carefree attitude about food.

When Spencer felt his stomach ache from fullness, he lay back on his bed and groaned. "Oh, God."

Calleigh remained sitting on the end of the bed, a dazed expression passing over her face. "I feel like I ate a bus."

"Yeah," he agreed. "A double-decker."

She nodded and turned her head to look at him. "Bed?"

He exhaled. "Bed."

*

A half an hour later, the room still smelling like fried food, they hit the lights and were plunged into darkness. Spencer rested his arms over the top cover, too hot to stay underneath. The silence that descended on them was almost absolute, if not for the kick of the air conditioner humming next to Calleigh's bed across the room, and Newton's slight wheezing every now and again.

There was something different about that silence at the end of a long day. That promise of sleep, slipping into a place where the worries of the world had a feeble, intangible hold on him. The darkness was a place he could hide. But it wasn't the same with Calleigh in the room. It wasn't the same knowing that it wasn't just him about to outrun the things that had chased him that day. He could tell just by her breathing, how it never slowed down nor seemed restful, that she was outrunning things, too.

Lost in this sea of thoughts, he found himself faintly aware of a slight yet repetitive squeaking sound sneaking through the emptiness, and eating into his consciousness.

"What the hell is that?" Calleigh asked, her voice deafening next to the slightness of the sound.

Spencer searched in the dark for Newton, figuring he was the likeliest culprit. But he'd curled up at the end of Calleigh's bed and the noise wasn't coming from that direction. He closed his eyes again, figuring he could ignore it.

As the moments passed, it picked up frequency. The noise was soon accompanied by a dull thump. The wall behind his headboard reverberated with the noise as it gradually got louder.

His eyes shot open with realization.

"Aw, nuts," Calleigh groaned.

"Come on!" he shouted, grabbing a pillow from where he'd tossed it on the floor and throwing it over his head to try and drown out the sound.

It didn't help. And it didn't stop.

"It would figure," Calleigh said with a sigh.

Spencer tossed the pillow back onto the floor, growling. "A few hours: that's all I'm asking for. Please!" he begged to the ceiling. And although one of the water stains looked vaguely like the outline of

Jesus, he received no celestial confirmation back nor did the noises from the other room cease.

Then another sound reached him, one that didn't seem right. Calleigh was giggling. It was squeaky and almost so slight next to the rumbling coming from the wall behind their heads. But it grew louder.

"How can you laugh?" he asked, in spite of the smirk that had found its way onto his face.

"How can you not?" she answered, losing herself in laughter. Newton looked at her with head cocked.

He shook his head, and at this point began to see her point. After all that they'd been through that day, it seemed as though some higher power owed them. But instead, they ended up with yet another strange and aggravating circumstance. Somehow, Spencer knew that there was just no escaping it. This was the karma for allowing Newton to pee on that red convertible earlier; bad karma in the form of wild thunderous sex echoing through the walls as if Greek gods were performing their carnal conquests in front of the mortal world without meaning to.

He couldn't keep it back any longer. He joined Calleigh laughing, losing himself in deep, belly-aching guffaws, and oxygen-starved howls. It stuck to his dreams like drops of golden honey, filling the night with blithe amusement that only seemed to dissipate when the sun rose the next morning. The light came off pale and pink like a warm mist blanketing the horizon.

After a shower and dressing into clean clothes, Calleigh took her turn in the bathroom. And as he'd suspected, she spent a long and seemingly luxurious time showering. He took that time to pick up some breakfast items from the little buffet in the tiny dining room off from the lobby of the motor inn.

Calleigh exited the bathroom soon after his return, smelling faintly of sweet green tea. She sat cross-legged at the end of her bed and bit into a blueberry muffin. "So," she said in between chewing, "any sign of the energetic couple next door this morning?"

"Actually, yes." Spencer took a sip of his coffee, reveling in the bold, hot flavor. "I caught them trying to sneak out of their room to check out early."

"Well? What were they like?"

"Not what you'd expect…"

She frowned.

"…An elderly couple from Minnesota."

Her eyebrows shot up. "Oh." They fell again. "Oooh…"

"Needless to say, I will never, ever ask my parents how they've spent their vacations ever again."

Calleigh chuckled as she chewed her muffin.

After they'd finished breakfast, they hit the open road again. It had cooled off a little from the previous day and there was a welcome warm breeze that mingled with their hair as they pulled back onto the interstate.

Spencer took the wheel first, a sliver of him still feeling guilty over the granola accusation the previous day. Despite eventually being able to drift off last night, his eyelids felt bowling ball-heavy and his stomach oddly full. He'd only been able to drink coffee and pick apart a bear claw that morning.

"Maybe that Chinese food wasn't such a great idea," he said at one point.

"I know what you mean," Calleigh remarked, gazing out her window. "I dreamed of giant crab rangoon trying to break into the hotel room. Imagine my surprise when I woke up and realized it was just our friends next door again."

He laughed.

She turned to him and snagged her water bottle from the cup holder. "What would you say to camping out tonight?"

His lip hung a little, the first excuse he could think of rising to his mind.

"I don't think I can handle another night of marshmallow mattresses and feisty seniors. Besides, it will save us some money."

He wanted to protest. But honestly, with how tired he was, he could sleep on any surface, even a pebbly rough patch of earth. He nodded and swallowed down any reservations at the sight of her satisfied smile.

The first hour seemed to slip by like that rush of air through the car windows. In memory, it seemed the time passed by quicker than the music on the radio. It was almost as if they existed in two separate universes. Somewhere in the back of his mind, a thought needled in his consciousness. He started remembering the camping trip he proposed taking with Lydia years ago. It had been camping in the sense that it was at a campground with other camp sites and other people, not off in the woods and away from civilization like it had been when his father had taken him.

He'd been in the kitchen trying to fix the coffeemaker but with no success. He'd gone into the living room where Lydia had laid across the couch with her book and gave her foot a gentle rub. "We should take some time off, drive out to the lake for a few days."

She hadn't even looked up from her book. "Are you joking?"

"No."

She'd clicked her tongue, and smiled that smile that meant she was more irritated than amused.

"I thought it would be fun," he'd added, despite knowing it would do little good.

"What happens if you have an episode?" Her tone was almost accusatory and it caught him off-guard.

"Then I take some pills and chill out in the tent. Honestly, I don't think I'm going to have one. It's the lake. What could happen?"

"There could be a bear…"

"A bear?" he'd said before she could finish.

"…or something else."

"Anyone in their right mind would have a panic attack if they saw a bear, Lyd."

She had suddenly thrown the book down into the crook of the couch cushions. "Can I please have a serious conversation with you for once?"

He'd stared at her. "What's this about?"

"I'm asking you what happens if you have an attack like the one you had a few weeks ago?"

He'd frowned.

"I would hate to be out there in the middle of nowhere, vulnerable like that, and not know what to do for you."

"We wouldn't be out in the middle of nowhere. There are others camping nearby..." Spencer slowed to a stop when he noticed her expression hadn't changed. He crouched down beside her on the couch and said, "What happened a few weeks ago was an entirely different situation. It was because of stress and work and...a whole bunch of things."

"It was only a short time ago, Spencer," she'd said, her tone a little too angry.

It made him set his teeth in frustration as he answered, "That's why I think it would be a good idea to take the vacation."

She didn't let up. "And I'm telling you it's too soon. You need to get back into a normal routine, try to make things work as they are. Running off to the woods for a weekend isn't going to help—"

He frowned. "Excuse me? "Running off"?"

"No. I didn't mean that. I meant..." She left the sentence hanging.

"You meant "running off"." He stood up and scoffed. "Is that what you think I want to do?"

"Well, I don't know, Spencer. You haven't really told me anything since the accident!" she yelled.

His throat burned as he stared at her. The sunlight splashed speckles of green over the furniture from the stained glass ornament hanging in the window. Next door, the dog was barking up a storm.

It had been the first of many fights to come.

Chapter 8

As Spencer backed out of the memory, he became vaguely aware of Calleigh shaking her head next to him. "Uh…" She shuffled the road atlas that was in her lap around and leaned over it, staring at the little squiggly lines. "Uh… Spence?"

"Yeah?"

"You remember that exit about twenty minutes back? The one that I asked you if we should take?"

He didn't. But he didn't want to tell her he hadn't really been paying attention for the last hour. Instead, he glanced at her out of the corner of his eye. "Were we supposed to take it?"

She didn't look at him. "I think we were."

"What do you mean "you think?"" he snapped, moving the car into one of the slower lanes.

"Well, the map is just a little confusing!" she yelled back. "After the tollbooth, there were, like, three possible exits. I asked you if you saw the exit we were supposed to take but you didn't answer."

"So you guessed?"

"I thought I picked the right one."

"You're the one with the map! You're supposed to tell *me* where to go!"

94

She put the atlas aside and glared at him. "It would help if you were actually paying attention to driving and weren't up in the clouds when I asked you a simple question."

He felt the tension rise in his chest as he spied the road signs for the next exit. "How do you know we're not going the right way?"

"The giant "Welcome to Michigan" sign that we just passed was a pretty good indicator."

"Shit," he muttered, pulling the Nissan off into the next exit.

"What are you doing?" Calleigh asked.

"I'm getting us turned around."

"There's a toll down here. We're going to have to pay to get in and then back out again."

"I don't care."

"Fine." She chuckled, an annoyed smile on her face. "It's your money."

He drove the car off the interstate and down the hill, circling like a corkscrew until they passed under the freeway and approached the line of tollbooths. There, Spencer quickly handed over a twenty to the old man in the window. The man tottered back into the booth and popped open his change drawer, painstakingly plucking each dollar bill and coin out until he had the correct change. He leaned over the gap to hand it all back to Spencer—and dropped it. Dollar bills flitted to the ground and change sprinkled on the pavement in a mess of jingles.

Spencer growled as he watched the various dimes, quarters,

and pennies roll away under the car and down the road. He got out and collected as many as he could, ushered on by the horn honking of the car behind him. The old man in the booth opened his door and started to come out but Spencer put a hand up. "I've got it. It's okay."

After collecting all he could find, he climbed back in the car and wordlessly pulled them through the tollbooth. Calleigh never said a word and Newton's happy panting was the only noise in the awkwardly silent space.

Spencer stopped the Nissan in the first place off the highway that he could find; a plant nursery, and climbed out. Calleigh rolled down her window. "If we can just get on the highway going the opposite way, I'm pretty sure I can find the exit we missed."

"Check the map again. I'd rather be positive than just "pretty sure"," he grumbled as he marched through the front door of the nursery.

Inside, he found himself surrounded by a swath of green, curling vines that seemed to drip from pots on high shelves and fronds that reached out into his path to trip him up. Sparkly streamers hung on the walls, looking like they'd been kept from old high school proms. The holographic purple and black letters somehow gave the place a garish feel.

They reminded him of the old flower shop he'd gone to when he was in high school. It had been located in the basement of an old elementary school back home. It was always dark inside, which prompted musings of whether or not their power bill had been paid.

Aside from all of the green, the only colors in that old shop seemed to come from assorted carnations in a vase on the counter and unclaimed corsages sadly staring up through the glass, their petals beginning to wilt. From then on, the store had kept a reputation as a plant nursing home rather than a nursery. The owners had cycled through a series of random businesses over the previous decade, everything from a catering business to a consignment clothing store to a video shop. They obviously weren't green thumbs either.

"Hello?" Spencer called the further he walked into the nursery.

"Be with you in a moment!" someone called from beyond the racks of gardening tools off to his right. Frankie Valli and the Four Seasons were playing from a tinny speaker over in the corner. It was a song that had played *at* his first high school prom in 1975. The memories came back in a reluctant tidal wave: the awkward robotic slow dance where he held his date, senior Jenny Tucci, at arms-length, the punch that nobody drank because the football jocks had already spiked it, and his rented tux that had smelled like white musk and mothballs. *Oh, the memories.*

"Hello, there!" a woman said as she appeared from the back room, spinning through a beaded curtain with a bag of fertilizer in her arms.

Squinty eyes, bronzed cheeks with dirt smudges here and there, and a tight-fitting button up shirt with crazy multi-colored squiggles, the woman looked as if she were trying to be Farah Fawcett with a gardener's twist. Her blonde hair had been hair-sprayed and styled into large sweeps away from her face with the aid of a curling iron, though the more prominent ones in the front ended up looking like an oversize mustache that's only rival could have been Hulk Hogan's handlebar.

Looks like not everyone escaped the seventies, he thought.

"Hi," he said as he choked down his laughter.

"Let me guess?" She put the bag down on the floor and a flirtatious smile crossed her face. "You're here to buy some flowers for your girlfriend?"

She had a very nice smile, which almost made him feel bad about his earlier comparisons. Almost.

"No, I'm actually in need of some good directions."

"Oh…" Her eyebrows rose. "Get turned around out there, did you?"

"Something like that."

She crossed to the counter and fumbled around underneath for a few folded maps. "Where are you headed?"

"I need to get back on the interstate, south to Indiana."

"Oh, that's simple enough." She dropped the maps and rounded the counter. "Come over here with me to the window."

He followed her, pushing through the indoor rainforest until they reached the glass wall that looked out on the street. It felt good to resurface from his plunge into the high school horror, if only to remember what the world looked like.

"Now, you're going to want to go down this road here for about…I don't know…quarter mile maybe? Until you get to the blue mailbox on the right corner."

"Okay." *Blue mailbox. Simple enough.*

"Then, you're going to want to turn right. Take that road for about six minutes."

He frowned. "Six?"

"Six exactly. Until you get to the tree."

""The tree?" What tree?"

"You know. *The* tree."

Spencer glanced outside again. There were dozens of trees on the sides of the roads. "What kind of tree are we talking about?"

"It's a big tree; a tall tree."

"As opposed to a short tree?" he let slip before he could keep himself.

She giggled. "You'll know what I mean when you get there."

He took a deep breath and held it. "Okay."

"Then, you'll take another right and follow that until you come to the intersection at the hill."

"Wait, I'm sorry. "The hill"?"

"Oh, come on! Everyone knows "The Hill"," she laughed.

"But I don't. Could you bear with me please? What hill?"

She leaned close to him, losing her smile. "The big one."

Spencer somehow kept from face-palming. *Should have expected that.*

*

Spencer left the greenhouse, his opinion of the rural population in Indiana having withered in light of Faux-Farah's directions.

Calleigh was stroking Newton's fur when he finally pulled his seatbelt across his lap and turned over the engine. "You know where we're going?"

"Apparently, we're looking for natural landmarks emphasized by their gigantism," he said, reversing the car out onto the road.

Calleigh's breath hitched and he didn't dare look at her for fear of completely losing his cool. "Like, lakes? Cliffs? Stuff like that?"

"Yeah."

As he drove the car down the road, he noticed the blue mailbox on the corner and turned right at it.

"She didn't have any better directions than that?" Calleigh scoffed.

"*She* is a Charlie's Angel's wannabe living in a terrarium decorated like my old high school prom. We're lucky she was even in the present enough to give directions."

He followed the road, his eyes shifting this way and that, trying to follow the flower shop lady's advice.

"What are we supposed to be looking for?" Calleigh asked. He almost didn't want to tell her.

"A big tree."

"You've got to be kidding me."

"Just look."

Right around the time, Spencer had counted six minutes in his head, he caught a strange shape off to the side of the road up ahead. A gleaming silver metal sculpture stood off in the rough on the left side of the road. It was almost as tall as the telephone pole nearby and accentuated by copper fruit that hung from the various branches.

"Oh." Calleigh nodded absentmindedly. "That tree."

Spencer took the turn to the right as they reached it. "My faith in the human race may not crumble after all."

"She couldn't have used a different descriptor though? Like a giant "metal" tree?"

Spencer glanced at the tree in the rearview mirror as it grew smaller and smaller. "I can't wait to see what this hill looks like."

*

Several hours later, they had found their way back into the correct state again and had resumed their drive along Interstate 80. The Illinois border had come and gone with rejoicing in the form of Newton happily chasing around a fly trapped in the backseat with him. According to the map, they were somewhere near Marsailles, near the middle of the state.

"I spy with my little eye…" said Calleigh, now in the driver's seat.

Spencer's gaze shifted over to her slowly. "No."

"You've been quiet ever since we left Michigan. I was just trying to give us something to do."

Road games such as I spy, the license plate game, and the ever popular Punch Buggy, were only entertaining in the most basic sense of the word. Then again, it had been a very long time since he'd spent this much time traveling on the road. His nerves were beginning to get the better of him.

The landscape had become flatter, emphasized by more fields of crops and seemingly endless stretches of tall grass. It was almost as though nothing existed for miles beyond that grass, swishing and swaying in the wind. It should have been comforting, but it just made him more edgy. Any time a semi-truck had appeared from an exit and merged onto the highway with them, he'd felt his heart rate practically triple. As much as he didn't enjoy the idea of playing a game meant to keep children from asking, "Are we there yet?", he was beginning to feel that if he didn't, he might start to ask the question, too.

"Fine."

Calleigh smiled and turned her attention back to the road. "I spy with my little eye something…green."

Spencer glared at her. "*Everything* is green!"

"Well, it's not supposed to be easy."

"You're starting to sound like Lydia," he muttered under his breath.

"Uh oh," Calleigh breathed, "I guess I stepped in it now."

He scoffed. "For all you know, that could have been a compliment."

"The moment a guy tells me that I remind him of his ex-wife, someone he separated from for shall we assume are irreconcilable differences, I think I'll just accept you were making me out to be the bad guy there."

He closed his eyes. "Don't do that. Don't assume that you know something about what happened between her and I."

"Then can you just play the damn game?" she said with a humorless chuckle.

Spencer sighed. "Fine."

"I spy with my little eye, something green."

Straightening in his seat, Spencer glanced in the rearview mirror at Newton, poised at one of the windows, his head leaning out into the open air. "Newton's collar."

Calleigh didn't respond. When he looked at her, he noticed her expression had shifted into disappointment. "That was it, wasn't it?"

She shrugged her shoulders. "You could have at least indulged me a little bit."

He shook his head with a smirk and looked out the window again. After a few moments, he said, "I didn't separate from her."

"Sorry?"

"I didn't separate from her. It was a mutual decision."

"What did she do that made things so unbearable?"

"She didn't do anything. Things just fell apart between the two of us."

"Please. You're not one of those types that's actually friends with your ex, are you?" She rolled up the window a little. The sound of the wind lessened.

"Why? Is that bad?"

"I just don't see the point in pretending that you like one

another if you don't."

He grimaced. "It's not about liking one another. It's about getting along so that things aren't awkward between the two of us."

"So you don't like her?"

"You're twisting my words around, Calleigh."

"And you're not answering any of my questions, Spencer."

"Didn't I say at the beginning of the trip that this topic was off limits?"

"It was until you brought it up." She shifted the car into the fast lane, zipping the Nissan around an old station wagon, something under its hood rattling incessantly.

"I was just getting the facts straight. I didn't mean for you to turn into a marriage counselor." He picked up his water bottle from the cup holder and twisted the lid off.

"Oh, forgive me." She put a hand to her chest mockingly. "I thought for a moment you actually wanted to have a meaningful conversation." She mumbled something more under her breath.

"Excuse me?"

"I said "not this chit-chatty crap we've been doling out for the last three days.""

He put the cap back on the water bottle without having taken a sip. "Well, I'm sorry that I tried to keep it light and didn't open up the journey with details about my messy divorce!"

"Ooh, so it was messy," Calleigh probed. "Even more of a reason why I should think that me being like her is a *compliment*."

Spencer shoved the water bottle back in the cup holder and stared out the window.

"You obviously need to talk about it, Spencer, so you might as well just—"

"No." He stared at her, his face sliding from frustration into numbness. "I'm not going to talk about it anymore."

"Suit yourself."

"I would, however, love to examine your sunny outlook on marriage." He felt a retaliatory smile slide over his face as he crossed his arms behind his head and leaned back.

"I've never been married, so there isn't much to tell," she said quickly.

"Well, something must have caused you to view divorce so ominously. Your parents divorced?"

"Nope."

"Brother? Sister?"

"Only child," she said this with some degree of triumph.

"Then, you are the last person to give advice when it comes to relationships," he reasoned. "Glad we got that out of the way."

"If anything, seeing how well my parents got along and tolerated one another should be a stunning example of why I give great relationship advice."

He looked at her hands on the steering wheel and scoffed. "I don't see a ring on your finger."

"That's because I don't plan on getting married."

He stopped before the next words left his mouth. "Why not?" he asked instead.

"Because I don't want to be tied down to anyone," she said, her tone shifting. It had become defensive now and Spencer knew he'd hit a nerve with the question. Despite knowing he should back off, he couldn't let her off that easily, not when she'd pried into his marriage only a few minutes prior.

"Free-spirited, huh? Another reason why you're a granola."

She sighed. "Not this again."

"You don't want to be "tied down"? What does that even mean?"

"It means what you think it means."

"I'm going to take a stab and say that it means you haven't had a serious relationship with anybody."

"That's more of a leap, wouldn't you say?" she growled. The car was going faster now, Calleigh shifting into the left lane to speed around the other cars in their way.

"You don't have any friends, do you?"

Her stare went blank for a moment, but only a moment. "I've got friends."

He thought back to their encounter with Patty in the diner in Pennsylvania. "You're a Debbie Washington, aren't you?"

"Macbeth didn't make me cry," Calleigh countered.

"I mean that you act superficial."

She chuckled. "That's rich coming from the guy who judges

everyone he meets by how they look."

"You get a kick out of telling me that I can't judge you if I don't know you but then you dodge all of my questions when I try to!"

Calleigh slowed the car down as they approached an exit from the turnpike and guided them onto it. "Spencer, what are the odds that we'll ever see each other after this trip?"

"You're the one who asked me to go, so you tell me?" he yelled.

Newton barked from the backseat.

"I figured there would be a one in one thousand chance, okay? So why should I tell you anything else, especially when all you want to do is use it as ammo for any future disagreements we might have!"

"Hello! Weren't you just the one who said you were tired of the "chit-chatty crap"?"

"We can have meaningful conversations about other topics that don't have to do with you or me," she shot back. They were driving along a country road now with nothing but stalks of corn and telephone poles for miles around. A feeling had crept into Spencer's gut that this wasn't the way they should be going but he was too busy trying to catch Calleigh in a lie.

"You are the biggest hypocrite in Illinois, Calleigh, which is saying something...because we're just passing through."

Her shoulders stiffened and her knuckles were practically white on the steering wheel. Everything about her body language suggested she was done with talking but Spencer didn't heed it. She'd kept enough secrets.

"The reason you were looking around for a stranger to go with you is because you didn't have any friends who would do it with you. Am I right?"

That finally did it. Calleigh pulled the car off the road and stopped. She spun at him with fury brewing like a storm in her eyes and said, "Fine! I have no friends. Is that what you want to hear? I'm friendless."

Spencer had thought it would satisfy him but instead it just made him feel emptier. "And why is that, Calleigh? Because it doesn't make sense to me."

"You know what doesn't make any sense to me?" she retaliated. "How does a guy suddenly start getting panic attacks five years ago for no reason whatsoever?"

He frowned. "It happens."

She shook her head. "No. Something *happened*, Spence."

"Don't try to change the subject. This isn't about me. This is about you and your reluctance to let anybody in."

She was silent for what seemed like an impossibly long amount of time. Then, she said, "And you are too scared to admit that you miss your wife."

The car was suddenly stifling. The breeze was gone and the way his temper was growing, he knew he wouldn't be able to stand the heat of that enclosed space for very much longer. He was almost trembling with the anger that surged through his system. It had been a mistake. He never should have thought that being trapped in a car with this woman would work out okay.

"All right," he said, opening the car door and climbing out. He'd been sitting in the car for so long that his legs had a hard time remembering what they were supposed to do when weight was put on them. "I've had it!"

"You've "had it"?" Calleigh parroted, a note of incredulity in her tone.

He walked to the trunk and slapped his palm on it. "Open it!"

Calleigh leaned out her window and stared back at him. "You can't be serious!"

He just stared. "Does this look like my joking face to you?"

"Is there a difference?" Calleigh retorted. The trunk popped open moments later.

Spencer hauled out his backpack and tossed it to the side of the road. It rolled down an embankment into a ditch. Growling, he slammed the trunk lid shut.

"Hey!" Calleigh yelled.

"Just go!" Spencer waved his arms. "I'll get a lift from someone and take the first fight back to Maine that I can!"

"The first flight?" Calleigh blew a raspberry. "Good luck finding an airport."

Spencer took a moment to survey his surroundings. It was green for miles and the only things that stood taller than the grass were the telephone poles lining the road. There was no sign of life anywhere. But his mind was made up.

"Then a bus, a train. Whatever I have to do to make sure I get as far away from this ludicrous situation as I have to."

He rounded to the passenger side window and leaned into it. "I mean, who in their right mind has the time to go gallivanting off to some pointless tree-hugger conference across the country without any obligations to work or family or whatever! Do you have any attachments? Is there anything rooting you anywhere?"

Calleigh stared straight through the windshield as if she hadn't heard him. But he saw her hands tightening around the steering wheel with every word he slung at her.

Newton yipped frantically from the backseat. His high-pitched yelping aggravated Spencer's already pounding headache.

"Shut up, Newton!" he finally yelled.

Calleigh spun toward Spencer, her blue eyes wild. "Fine, Spencer! You want to go? I'll gladly leave you here."

She wrenched the shifter into gear. Spencer barely had enough time to get out of the way before she slammed her foot on the accelerator and took off down the road, a dirt cloud consuming him in the car's wake. By the time it cleared, the Nissan was far down the road. For a few moments, he thought he almost saw Newton in the back window, his tongue not lolling out of his mouth for once. The car became a small red spot and grew smaller and smaller until it was finally gone in the haze.

Spencer looked around and sighed. Finally, silence. He

collected his backpack from the ditch, hoisted it on his back, and started down the road. Over the next couple hours, he realized how much he truly loathed the quiet.

Chapter 9

An Eastern Whip-poor-will called across the blue sky as Spencer traipsed down the side of the empty road. He'd been keeping time the further he'd walked; five minutes, ten minutes…twenty. He gave up and settled his sights on the horizon, searching for something that looked man-made besides the telephone poles. Nothing.

Apparently, Calleigh had left him in the most secluded place in all of Illinois before driving off in a blast of dirt clouds. He wondered if she was back on the interstate now, speeding along toward Oregon with Newton happily perched to look out the front passenger side window.

"It's for the best," he said aloud. "I'd have probably gone insane before we got there anyway."

He continued on for another few minutes until a sound interrupted the silence, a faint low hum of an approaching vehicle, dirt crunching beneath tires. Spencer turned around. Not a single car had driven by in the last half an hour and his feet were getting tired. His shoes were old, but he'd brought them because they were comfortable in that broken-in, customized kind of way. He hadn't expected to be walking a marathon in them on the trip.

He noticed a truck approaching from behind him though it was still very far away. Spencer immediately stuck out his thumb. This guy *had* to pick him up. But as the haze cleared and the truck grew closer, Spencer allowed his sunglasses to slide down his nose. The truck pulled up alongside him. A burly man in a green plaid shirt and cowboy hat leaned over toward the passenger window. "Need a ride?" he called.

Spencer opened his mouth. When he did so, a horrifying stench permeated his senses. It went beyond any terrible odor he'd ever experienced in his entire life. Not even that weekend as a kid cleaning a public facility's toilets as part of community service for stealing a candy bar compared to the intrusive, pore-clogging stench that emanated from that truck. And then his eyes fell on the decal plastered over the car door: Department of Transportation: Del's Taxidermy. *Of all the cars in the state of Illinois…*

"Mister? I said, do you need a ride?"

Walk until my shoes catch fire or endure an at most ten minute ride in Charon's pickup? The decision was more difficult to make than it should have been.

"Yeah, I do."

The man popped open the side door with a smile and said, "Climb on in!"

Spencer stepped up into the truck cab. There he found himself in a veritable junk-laden netherworld of oil-streaked car parts, crumpled soda cans, and many rags with questionable stains.

The driver had a thick build with big cheeks and small blue

eyes, a face Lydia would have called "a babyface". In his worn jeans, tall rubber boots, and plaid shirt, he looked like someone Spencer would have seen back in Maine if not for the cowboy hat with the snake skin band. He shoved a meaty hand at Spencer which he took with some trepidation. "Name's Arnie."

"You mean you're not Del?"

Arnie laughed and returned his hand to the gear shift. "Hell no! Del doesn't drive the trucks. The poor sons a' bitches he employs do that!"

Spencer's upper lip curled without his knowledge. "Oh. Ha ha…"

Arnie put the truck in gear and pulled back onto the road, the engine sounding as though it was missing a few key nuts and bolts as something under the hood clanked. Spencer remembered these old trucks from the early sixties and still saw a few driving around back home in Maine. This one however, definitely sounded worse for wear.

"So, where you headed?" Arnie asked.

"The nearest airport," Spencer replied.

"Well, there's plenty of 'em around these parts, though most are abandoned."

Spencer sighed. "Then I just need to get to the nearest hotel. I'll figure out something from there."

"Did yer wife kick you out or something?" Arnie asked, eyeing Spencer's pack in his lap.

Spencer shook his head. "I was traveling west with a friend.

114

Things went sour."

A large smile wrapped on Arnie's face. "A *girl* friend?"

Spencer squinted. "A friend who happens to be a girl, but nothing more than that."

"Oh, sure. I just figured it had to be a woman is all."

"Why is that?"

"Because if two fellas were traveling across country, a little fight wouldn't be enough to end the trip. A girl on the other hand... she gets emotional and things can't be simple."

Despite the fact that Arnie had almost hit the problem right on the nose, Spencer refused to allow him that point. "Would you mind dropping me off at the nearest hotel?"

"Sure thing. It's in Grand Ridge."

"How far is that?"

"About fifteen miles. Not too far."

Spencer let out a stale breath. "Good."

"But hey listen," Arnie said, and that was all it took to make the hope in Spencer's chest deflate once again.

"Yeah?"

"I've really got to take care of a few runs while I'm out here. The DOT has us do these runs based on tips people have called in. I've got a few on here that have been cooking for days and they need to be done. You think you could sit tight while I go collect a few?"

No! I don't want to be trapped in a truck while you huck dead animal pancakes in the back of it! Spencer wanted to exclaim. But he knew he couldn't. This guy had picked him up to be nice. And he was willing to give him a ride back to a hotel. *I could lie, say that I have somewhere I need to be by a certain time*, he thought. But he knew Arnie wouldn't believe him. He had no good reason. As much as Spencer didn't want to, he found himself nodding.

"Great," Arnie said, downshifting as they reached a corner and turned left. "It shouldn't take too, too long."

Famous last words, Spencer thought as they began down another straight country road.

*

It wasn't too much longer until they came across the first "pick-up". Spencer saw it lying to the side of their lane, just barely over the white line.

Arnie left the truck running and climbed out of the cab. "Let's see what we've got here." He collected a small shovel and a bucket from the back of the truck and strode over to the road kill. Spencer watched him as he stopped near it and crouched down, looking it over from all sides. "Looks like a muskrat," he called back.

Spencer leaned out the car window and let his shades slip down to the end of his nose. Whatever it was left on the road didn't look like it had much of a shape left.

Arnie plunked the shovel onto the pavement and gently tried to slide it under the animal. "It's been out here so long, even the flies don't want it."

Spencer's mouth straightened as he nodded.

116

The shovel stuck about half way under the muskrat. Arnie pulled the shovel back out and quickly jerked it back under. Spencer looked away just in time, hearing the burnt flesh tear from the pavement. He leaned back inside the truck. "I knew this was going to be a bad afternoon," he said to himself.

After a few more scrapes, Arnie dropped the muskrat into the bucket and started back to the truck. As he went by the window, the smell invaded the cab full on. Spencer put his arm over his nose. It didn't help.

Arnie tossed the shovel into the truck and climbed in. One glance at Spencer sent him laughing, his girth shaking the truck. "Sorry about the smell. I forget that other people aren't used to it. I'm around it every day so I don't even notice now."

Spencer tried to say something but just ended up coughing.

"Right, onto the next one. We'll get this done so we can get you back to town." The truck took off down the road once more.

As the afternoon light slowly draped over the golden and green fields, the heat seemed to intensify. The truck was roasting, even with the windows open. There wasn't a hint of a breeze out today and it just made the stench in the truck bed that much more unbearable. Over the next half an hour, Arnie added a ground squirrel, a juvenile brown snake, a fox snake, and a woodpecker. All in all, Spencer had expected worse.

But as they rounded the corner onto a dirt road leading to an abandoned farm, Arnie stopped the truck short in the middle of the road.

Spencer snapped out of his daze and stared at Arnie. "What's going on?"

"Son of a bitch," Arnie muttered under his breath as he jumped out of the cab and slammed the door behind him. He quickly grabbed a pair of thick rubber gloves from the back of the truck. And then he slid out something that made Spencer's breath catch; a rifle.

His eyes followed Arnie as he started down the road ahead of them. Then he saw it. There was a red fox lying in the middle of the road, squirming around frantically. He could see the small stain of blood in the dirt and knew the animal had been hit. And though he knew what was coming, he still wasn't prepared for it. The moment that Arnie was close enough, he clicked the safety off on the rifle, chambered a round, and shot the fox without a moment to spare. The crack of gunfire echoed across the sky.

A cloud passed over the sun and suddenly dulled all of the colors of the countryside. Spencer couldn't help but stare, his heart beating so loud he could hear it over Arnie who was shouting to him. Spencer pulled the door handle and pushed out. He had to force himself to remember how to walk as he hesitantly grew closer to Arnie. "What'd you say?"

"I said, "Damn kids."" He held up a dirt smudged beer can. "Found it nearby. This road heads to an abandoned farm. It's a place that some of the kids around here go to drink, maybe do drugs..."

Spencer came within a few feet of the fox and stopped, unable to look at it. "It was an accident," he said, a shard of him feeling as if he were defending not the kids but himself in some way. After all, he was a defense lawyer. It was what he made a living at. But this time, he immediately hated himself for it. He looked up at Arnie and found that the driver was shaking his head.

"See these skid marks back here?" He pointed to a spot in the dirt just a few feet from Spencer. "Those kids were heading straight until they saw the fox. They swerved there, cut across the road and hit it."

Spencer's stomach dropped like a stone. All he could think of to say was, "Kids are stupid."

Arnie slung the rifle over his shoulder and picked up the fox in his gloved hands. "People are stupid." He walked passed Spencer as he returned to the truck.

*

Night was falling on the fields in a pale purple veil as Arnie finally turned the truck to head toward Grand Ridge. Spencer stared ahead at the blue mist on the horizon, unsure exactly how he felt. His eyelids were heavy but a melancholy twinge in his head had kept them from closing. He felt pain around the rims. His skin was clammy from the sweat and the dipping temperature of evening made the tiny hairs on his arms stand. Oddly enough, he wasn't thinking about the experience he'd just endured, the stench of all the road-kill in the back of the truck, or even the fox that Arnie had put out of its misery. He was thinking about getting on a plane and returning home. He was thinking about how much he was going to dread returning to his apartment and the silence that waited for him there.

Those expectations however skidded to a halt when he noticed a flickering orange light emanating from off the road alongside an abandoned gas station. He squinted as the truck got closer. Parked on the side of the road was a red Nissan, the passenger side mirror missing. Sitting in front of the fire near a pitched tent was one person.

"Can you let me out up here?" Spencer asked, his voice distant.

Arnie raised an eyebrow. "I thought you wanted to get into a hotel?"

"It's okay," he said. "I've caught up with my ride."

Arnie glanced at the fire off the side of the road and nodded. He pulled the truck to the side of the road near Calleigh's car. Spencer shook hands with Arnie. "Thanks again for the ride."

"It was no problem. Now, go make up with your friend that just happens to be a girl."

Spencer scoffed as he climbed out of the truck and it rumbled off down the road, soon fading into the haze in the distance. Putting his hands in his pockets, Spencer strode down through the grass toward Calleigh's camp.

She was sitting on her cooler, staring at him as he got closer.

Newton appeared from inside the tent, yipping gleefully as he waddled over toward Spencer. He only got a few steps however before he whined and shook his head with a sudden exhale. Calleigh, too, had crinkled up her nose.

"Hi," he said.

"Hey," she managed, closing her eyes. "You stink."

"I know." He got a little closer until he felt the slightest traces of heat from the fire. "I just spent the last couple hours in a DOT highway truck picking up road-kill."

Calleigh's eyes widened. "That sounds...like it was fun."

"Oh, it was heaps of fun." He smirked but soon lost it when he noticed that Calleigh wasn't smiling. "Do you mind if I join you?"

She waved toward the spot in front of him and he promptly sat. "Just be careful about snakes," she added. "There's a lot of them out here."

He glanced around him warily. "Thanks. I've seen them."

"Have a sudden change of heart?" she asked, digging into her bag next to her.

"One that can only come from spending the day in a sweaty, stinky DOT truck," he said with a smile.

Calleigh hummed but said nothing.

"I said some pretty bad things, Calleigh."

She clicked her tongue. "Oh, I know."

He tilted his head back and looked up at the sky, which was still in the blend between black and blue. "It's like a defense mechanism and it's automatic."

"Not good with apologies, are you?"

Spencer stared at her. "I'm sorry."

She scoffed. "Well, I did grill you pretty hard about your ex-wife if that's any consolation."

He shook his head. "I shouldn't have broached the subject."

"But she's been on your mind ever since we left Maine," Calleigh said, "hasn't she?"

"Yeah," he admitted, picking up a stick from the grass beside him.

Calleigh pulled a couple cans out of her bag and stared at him a moment while he drew stick figures in the dirt. "Any time you want to talk—"

"No. I mean…thanks, but, I think I'll just leave this one alone, okay?"

"Fair enough," she agreed. "Well, I was just about to cook up some franks and beans. You in?"

Spencer's thoughts began to turn back to the adventure he'd just undergone in the DOT truck but he stopped himself short. "Sure."

Calleigh tossed him the can of beans and a can opener. "You get to do the hard work then," she said with a smile.

"I feel like a pioneer already," he remarked, setting to work.

"The pioneers didn't have can openers."

Newton ruffed as if in agreement.

He eyed the dog. "You don't have to back her up, you know."

Chapter 10

A steady blanket of sunshine bled into the deep orange fabric of the tent when Spencer awoke. He let a hand slide over his face and sighed happily when he didn't make contact with anything resembling a flattened, pincer-tailed earwig body. He climbed out from the pile of blankets and hastily pulled them back around him again. It was surprisingly chilly. He sniffed his undershirt and cringed. It still smelled like roadkill. Calleigh had made him put his shorts and button-up shirt outside to air out the night before, claiming she couldn't breathe until he did so.

At first, he hadn't been sure about sharing a tent with Calleigh. It was smaller than he'd expected and there was barely enough room for the both of them to squeeze in together and zip up the fly. It had been a while since he'd shared sleeping space with anyone either, which made it only seem more uncomfortable. And it didn't help that Newton had firmly wedged his sausage body between the two of them, taking up even more precious space. But at least there hadn't been any creepy crawlies or feelings of intruding into one another's personal room.

Hoisting on a pair of shorts over his boxers, he poked his head outside the tent. A fog hazed over the woods, making them a blur of green moss beneath the blue sky. The grass was dewy and warm underfoot as he stepped out.

Calleigh was hunched near her camp stove, boiling some water for coffee. "Morning," she called and glanced over her shoulder. "You sleep well?"

He picked up his sneakers and shook them, making sure nothing had nested inside during the night. "Yeah. Aside from you snoring."

"Me? Snore?" She put a hand to her chest. "I'm as quiet as a mouse when I sleep."

He sat at the opening of the tent and pulled on his socks and shoes. "Well, last night, it sounded like a mouse operating a rototiller."

"You can blame Newton." She turned to look at the corgi. He was standing on a rock nearby, his eyes glued to a white moth fluttering around him precariously.

Spencer finished tying his shoes and joined Calleigh by the camp stove. "Is that coffee you've got going?"

She nodded. "I made it extra strong."

"Ah, sweet nectar of the wayfaring gods."

"Wow, I must be doing well. Last night, I actually had you apologizing. This morning, I'm a deity."

"I wasn't referring to you," he said, matter-of-factly, staring toward the road. "I was referring to the people who picked the beans and washed them and processed them…"

"I don't think I've ever heard you so appreciative of the

124

working class before," Calleigh said in amazement.

"Hey, I'm part of the working class, too."

"You stand in a court room and defend a guy who crashes people's cars!"

"Sometimes my clients are actually innocent."

"Crashes people's cars so badly that they catch on fire," she added, taking the percolator off the camp stove.

He opened his mouth to say something when another thought crossed his mind. "When did I say I didn't have respect for the working class?"

Calleigh raised her eyebrows. "Oh, it was implied."

"When?"

"At Patty's Diner. You thought we would be eating roadkill for breakfast."

He stared at her and followed her eyes over to his previous day's clothes still spread off on the ground near the tent to air out. Both the shirt and shorts were soaked through by the morning dew. He returned his eyes to her. "The irony isn't lost on me."

Calleigh pulled two cups out of her bag. "Good."

Thinking it better to end the disagreement before she could one up him again, he moved back over to the tent to collect his bag from inside.

"You know," Calleigh called, just as he got to the opening, "if I'm part of the working class, doesn't that make me kind of a—"

"No."

"It's fine," she answered. "I wouldn't want you sacrificing animals in my name anyway."

"I can just sacrifice my shirt instead," he remarked, stepping inside.

After taking down the tent and packing up the car, they stood by the side of the road sipping their coffee. Calleigh had pulled out the road map and spread it out across the hood of the Nissan to plot their route. Because of yesterday's snag, she'd come up with the idea that instead of camping anywhere, they'd just take shifts driving through the night in order to make up for their lost time. Though a lingering feeling in Spencer's mind had objected to it at first, he'd agreed to the plan. They'd both thrown enough of a tantrum the day before and they were running out of time to make it to the conference before it started.

After they'd confirmed their route and folded up the map, Calleigh shut Newton into the backseat of the car. As she turned to look over their camp site once more, she pointed to something on the ground. "Don't forget your sacrificial garments."

Spencer turned. His shirt and shorts were still lying across the grass. He jogged over to them and leaned down, picking up the shirt. *Totally soaked through*, he thought, waving it through the air with a quick snap. Water sprayed over him. "Great," he mumbled, reaching down to get the shorts.

Movement from one of the legs stopped him. He straightened and almost as soon as he did, he caught sight of a long serpentine head emerging from the waist line. "Oh!" he yelled, jumping back several steps.

"What?" Calleigh called from the car.

"There, uh…there appears to be a snake in my shorts."

Calleigh laughed. "So that's what you call your—"

"Calleigh!" he cut her off. "I'm serious."

She shut the car door and started down toward him. She started to walk passed him, her head leaning to one side. "Where is it?"

He put an arm in front of her. "Not too close." He pointed.

She squinted until she finally saw the mottled black head. "Ohhh."

""Ohhh"? What is "Ohhh"?"

"That looks like a bullsnake," she said.

"Is it poisonous?"

She shook her head. "I can't get a very good look at it though. I might be wrong." She glanced at him. "Any ideas?"

He scoffed. "No! What about you? Aren't you the deity of road-travel? Friend to all the animals?"

"I've never been much good with snakes," she admitted.

"What about Newton?" Spencer asked, glancing back at the car. "Can't we just sic him on the thing?"

"Not if it's poisonous!" she snapped at him.

The snake hissed as it nestled further into the shorts. Both of them took a cautionary step back.

"Do you need those shorts?"

"In most circumstances, I'd say no. But…"

"But?"

"I forgot to take out my wallet last night."

Calleigh's blue eyes widened. "Great."

"Yeah."

She focused on the snake's head again. "It has to be a bullsnake."

Spencer cocked his head. "Why?"

"Because the poisonous snake that it looks like only lives in the southern part of the state."

"Well, that's a relief."

She paused. "I'm pretty sure anyway."

"You're pretty sure?"

"I'm almost positive."

He put a hand over his eyes. "About as sure as you were when we ended up in Michigan?"

She nodded as she took a step back and grabbed a charred stick from last night's fire pit.

Spencer eyed the stick. "What are you going to do with that; beat it to death?"

"I had something a little less violent in mind," Calleigh said. She dipped the stick down toward the bottom of the pair of shorts and gently poked at the snake. With a loud hiss, the creature slid forward until its head disappeared into the grass a bit. Then, she prodded the stick under the snake's middle and carefully lifted.

The snake suddenly lunged at the stick, mouth wide.

128

Calleigh shrieked and dropped it.

Spencer jumped back. "You've pissed him off now."

Instead of attacking again, the snake slithered off further into the grass. Both Calleigh and Spencer kept their eyes on it until it was a good distance away. Then, he snagged the shorts.

"The thing probably laid eggs in here," he said, shaking them out.

Calleigh rolled her eyes as she started back to the car. "I highly doubt it."

He followed, plucking his wallet from the back pocket of the shorts and sliding it into his own. "I'm not sure I'm going to be able to wear these again."

"Why not? I thought snakes and lawyers were practically cousins," Calleigh quipped, as she climbed in the car.

He straightened. "When you were a kid, did a lawyer run over your puppy or something?"

She chuckled and said, "Just so you know, you're proving me wrong, Spence."

He climbed in the car and took his place behind the wheel. "All right, let's go."

He turned the key. The engine whined in a valiant effort to turn over but then coughed and sputtered out. He frowned as he gave it another try. This time, the engine fired up. "What was that about?"

"It does that sometimes."

"It hasn't done that any other time this trip."

"Sure it has," Calleigh said. "It's an old car. It's been repaired so many times that there's practically no original parts except for the engine and the frame."

"That's very reassuring," he remarked, pulling them out onto the road. "At least we're moving."

He directed the Nissan through the hot dusty side roads until they reached pavement once more. The sun painted shadows over the fields, stalks of wheat like glistening whiskers against the brilliant rays. Not too long after, they found themselves back on the interstate in a mass of other passenger cars, cruising toward the border of Iowa.

They stopped once at a gas station to clean up. "You're starting to look like Van Gough," Calleigh said to him as they got out of the car.

"Yeah," he agreed. He was looking pretty scraggily. He ventured into the men's room and unpacked his shaving kit, while Calleigh bought them breakfast. He wasn't surprised to see that he wasn't alone. There was another guy with white foam covering his chin, dragging a razor across it. He nodded to Spencer and they both continued their routines, a strange unspoken bond established toward this essential road trip happenstance.

Calleigh smiled as he stepped out and tossed him a paper bag. The warm smell of fried hash browns invaded his senses and set his stomach growling. "You read my mind."

"Fried food always tastes good first thing in the morning," she agreed, biting into her own.

"You mean you're not going to eat an apple and some yogurt?"

"There are mornings for that. This isn't one of them."

They finished up breakfast and returned to the car. Iowa wasn't a massively different terrain as Spencer had expected. More wide open fields of grains, vegetables, and corn that seemed to vanish back beyond the horizon. The sky was a rich cornflower blue that curved over them like a bowl, just as it had done when Spencer had first driven to Calleigh's apartment days ago in Maine. Except now, despite feeling small, he wasn't uncomfortable with it. It seemed right.

The traffic in Iowa gave way to some of the stranger sights of their trip. They passed an SUV that had been painted over to look like a mural of a night sky and a lake surrounded by woods. On one of the doors there was a decal that read, Iowa Cryptid Society with a large blue sea serpent painted rudimentarily through the logo.

"The Loch Ness Monster apparently has a cousin that lives in Iowa," Calleigh remarked.

"It's the country cousin of Nessie," Spencer said, "It wears a straw hat and chews on a blade of grass just before it attacks."

"Wow, how trite of you," Calleigh laughed.

"And if you're not careful, it will throw pieces of shucked corn at you."

She stared at him. "Shucked corn?"

"That or potatoes."

"That's Idaho, you idiot."

They passed defunct gas stations, the windows broken out and interiors darkened. Old barns zoomed by, their weathered grey wood being further bleached by the sun, and houses that sat back several yards from the road. The way the sun cast them into shadow made them seem figments of Spencer's imagination, as if they were part of a past that had left its memories behind like streaks of water colors on the Iowan canvas.

"Just think," Calleigh muttered, "if the zombie apocalypse happened, you'd never know it out here."

Spencer scoffed. "Who's being trite now?"

She stared out her window. "I'm just saying it's pretty quiet. But it's kind of nice."

He nodded. "And then you see the bodies start to rise in the fields."

She hit his arm playfully.

"You know, now that you mention it, getting attacked by a farmer zombie would probably be the scariest thing imaginable," Spencer said, grabbing his water bottle and unsuccessfully attempting to unscrew the cap.

Calleigh took it from him and did it. "As opposed to being attacked by a zombie in general?"

"Think about it," he said, accepting his water from her and taking a sip. "The coveralls, the pitchforks…"

"The being un-dead…" Calleigh added.

"Then again, a zombie clown would be just as frightening."

"Oh, you're one of those people."

He turned, his eyes wide. "Clowns are scary! All that make-up making them look eternally happy, balloon tricks, poofy hair…"

Calleigh bit her lip to keep from laughing. "…The big shoes."

"My parents took me to a circus once when I was a kid. It was one of those traveling ones with the lion tamer, acrobats, elephants—"

Calleigh cut him off. "Basically, a circus."

"—And lots of clowns; too many, in fact. They had this area where you could leave your kids to get their faces painted with some clowns so you could go off and get your chili dogs and play games. My parents left me with Persnickety and Delbert while they went off to see the 4H booths. It was the most horrible experience of my life."

He glanced over. Calleigh was giggling so hard, she was having trouble breathing.

Spencer rolled his eyes.

She managed to get herself under control. "That must have been horrible for you," she said, barely containing her grin.

"By the time, they got back, I looked like a mini Bozo and I'd wet myself from the terror."

"Aw." Calleigh put her hand on his shoulder.

"Never again, I tell you."

Houses and trees began appearing more and more as they closed in on Des Moines.

"Civilization!" Spencer yelled, as he saw a small house with a garage appear over a rise.

"You know, I think you're being a little rough on Iowa,"

Calleigh said, "considering that we come from Maine."

"That's why I don't feel so guilty."

"It's probably not so different from Maine when you think about it."

"Maine gets such a bad rap from all of the other states because it's so far north! People just assume we're part of Canada and that we all wear flannel. We all live out in the backwoods, know how to ride a moose, and don't have running water."

"So then, maybe treating Iowa so stereotypically isn't such a great idea after all," she said.

"It's harmless, Calleigh. It's not like I'm proclaiming over their radio that they're a bunch of corn-obsessed farmer zombies."

Calleigh shook her head. "That would be a first."

*

Spencer and Calleigh stopped on the side of the road just before hitting Des Moines and stretched. Calleigh took Newton for a long walk while Spencer regarded the directions. They were only about a couple hours away from hitting the Nebraska border and had reached the midpoint of their journey across the country. Spencer could hardly believe that everything they'd already been through had only been one half of their trip. It had seemed like a week already.

He let Calleigh take the wheel when they got back on the road once more. After negotiating the twists and turns of Urbandale and Clive, they were once again on a straight road heading toward Nebraska. Spencer had just begun to relax into the passenger seat when the radio suddenly shut off.

He frowned. "What happened? We lose the signal from the station or something?"

Calleigh twisted the dial but nothing happened. There wasn't even any static.

"What's going on?"

The car suddenly began to decelerate.

"I don't think we need to slow down," he said.

"I'm not," Calleigh growled, stomping on the gas pedal. She flicked on the blinker which did nothing as she slowly pulled them off to the side of the road. The car rolled for a few more feet before coming to a dead stop. In a nearby tree, a crow cawed.

"No, no, no…" Calleigh said, shutting off the engine and trying to turn it over again. Something clicked but nothing else happened.

Spencer frowned. "It's okay. It always does this, doesn't it?"

Calleigh gave him a look. "Hardy, har, har. I think the battery died."

"Are you sure it wasn't the alternator?"

"I'm praying it wasn't." Calleigh popped the hood and climbed out of the car.

She slid her fingers into the space under the hood and hoisted it up to block his view from the windshield. He got out after her. Newton poked his head out the window, panting.

"The battery's dead," she announced, as Spencer came around the front. "We should see if someone can give us a jump. That would tell us if the alternator went."

He scoffed. "Good luck getting someone to pull over."

Almost immediately after the words had left his mouth, a 4x4 pick-up truck pulled off in front of them and a man climbed out, leaving his engine running.

"He looks like the real life version of Elmer Fudd," Spencer remarked quietly.

Calleigh elbowed him in the ribs before she stepped out to greet him. The man, wearing plaid and donning Fudd's signature hat, agreed to give their battery a boost. But after he'd attached the cables and let the truck run for a while, the battery stayed flat.

"Thanks anyway!" Calleigh called as the man got back in his truck and pulled back out into traffic. "Shit..."

"I'll call Triple A," Spencer said, pulling out his phone.

The next half hour was spent leaning against the car in the intense summer heat, watching the traffic race by as they waited for the tow truck to arrive. When Spencer was sure that the sweat had completely soaked his shirt, it came. They shared the cab with a skinny kid who looked no older than twelve and probably, most assuredly shouldn't have been driving the car. Calleigh was squeezed into the middle which only seemed to excite their under-age chauffeur all the more. Spencer let his arm hang out the window with Newton comfortably situated on his lap as the tow truck brought them back into town. Finally, they stopped at an auto repair shop on the corner of one of the main streets.

There were cars parked in every available spot in the lot, most which looked like they hadn't moved in quite some time. The hood was raised on the closest one to them, a giant hole staring up at them where the engine should have been. *We're going to be here for a while,* Spencer thought as they got out of the tow truck and walked inside to the waiting room, plopped into some sticky vinyl seats, and waited.

They spent the next hour in silence, listening to the whining of the air conditioner and the distant mechanical whirs from the garage next door. They saw the mechanic only once, a middle-aged guy wearing a navy jumpsuit, with unruly black hair. Calleigh crossed and uncrossed her legs, and rubbed her eyes. He didn't have to ask to know how frustrated she was. Years ago when the muffler had fallen off his Lexus following an incident with road debris, he had spent hours pacing the shop awaiting the repairman's prognosis. Except that this time, they were stranded out in the middle of nowhere and Calleigh's car was the only way out.

The technician finally appeared from the slate grey door that connected to the workshop, wiping his grease-coated hands with a rag.

"Well, your alternator's shot," he said, tossing the rag onto the counter.

Calleigh tipped her head back and said a quiet curse that only Spencer heard. She stood and met the repairman at the counter. "How much is it going to be to fix?"

The repairman's lips formed a straight line. "I've got to call around and see if I can find one that can replace it. Otherwise, I'd have to order one straight from the factory. We could be talking upwards of three hundred, possibly four."

Spencer watched the shock slowly fill Calleigh's eyes and he knew instinctively she didn't have that kind of money. Any money she'd had saved up had been for this trip alone. He stood up. "Why don't you start calling some places about that alternator?" Spencer said gently to the repairman. "We're going to get something to eat. Anywhere close by we can go?"

He pointed out the window. "There's a little diner across the street. Great burgers."

"Thanks."

Spencer grabbed Newton's leash and put his arm around Calleigh, guiding her out the door.

The diner was poorly lit and was nearly empty at that odd hour in the afternoon. A television up in the corner of the room was broadcasting a local program of a lady filming a vole in her backyard. The few people in the diner were all absorbed in watching it, slowly chewing their food.

Apparently this lady knows how to provide enthralling commentary, Spencer thought.

Calleigh sipped at her lemonade, her eyes glued to the utensils rolled in a napkin.

"I don't know what to do," she said, pushing the glass aside. "I didn't expect this to happen."

"No one expects their car to die on them."

"I just…" Her sentence drifted off as she grabbed the lemonade again and took a long sip.

He propped an elbow on the table and frowned. "Do you have enough to fix it?"

Her face went blank for a moment. He'd seen her apartment. The furniture was old as were most of the appliances. The Nissan was over twenty years old. Of course she didn't have the money. But instead of confirming his suspicions, she slowly nodded. "If I pull some money out of my savings, I might have just enough."

Suddenly, Spencer's phone buzzed in his pocket. It was only the second time it had gone off the entire trip, the first being a wrong number from a collection agency looking for Suzy Stone. "Order me a burger, will ya? I'll be right back."

He only caught a slight nod from her as he turned and pushed out the front door of the diner into the heat of the day. The number that flashed on the little screen wasn't one he recognized. He flipped open the phone. "Hello?"

"I am sitting here in your office, Mr. Teel," a distinctly French voice said, his tone containing the faintest traces of prissiness. "And you are not here!"

Spencer ground his teeth. He could picture his client, Donat LeRoy, in his neat little office, sitting in *his* roller chair, feet propped up on *his* desk, as if he were king of Spencer's castle. "Yeah, well, a few days ago, Mr. LeRoy, I was in the same boat. I was sitting at a deposition that you were supposed to be at and failed to show up to."

"When I called your office, zey told me zat you were on vacation. I told zem zat couldn't possibly be true. Zey said, "But yes. He is!""

"Sounds like you guys said a lot."

"Mais oui! And I drove over here to find zat zey were speaking ze truth."

Spencer scratched his head. "Yeah, you'll find that we lawyers aren't necessarily impeccable liars all the time."

"Which brings me to question why you are taking a vacation in ze middle of my case?" LeRoy growled.

"I think you have as much to answer for as I do, Mr. LeRoy: leaving unannounced the day before your second deposition, you're only shot at getting out of this mess without having to go to court."

"I had urgent business to attend to. I go where I'm needed."

Spencer rolled his eyes.

"You on ze ozer hand…zat's a different matter. Zey told me zat you would be gone for two weeks. Zat is…impardonnable!"

"Listen, I'm sorry but the court date has already been set. I left the case work with one of my other advisors. She's familiarized herself with the case and can be there for you as a resource if you have any quest—"

"I hired you!" he shouted. "Not one of your laquais!"

"Well, until I get back, one of my "laquais" is who you're going to have," Spencer said.

"I demand you fly back here immediately!"

"And when I get back there, are you going to disappear again? Go for a nice jaunt off to Minneapolis while I get stuck making excuses for you again?"

LeRoy chuckled. "Do you speak to all of your clients like zis?"

"I don't need to. They know better than to run off on impromptu trips."

"As should you," LeRoy snarled. "You're fired."

Spencer's face dropped. "You're kidding, right? You're going to cut me loose when you are about to go to trial; after my office has spent the last two months working this for you?"

"You've done nothing for me. A skilled solicitor would have been able to get zis entire case dismissed, but not you. You're exactly ze same as most Americans: driven by money but absolutely inept to zeir customer's necessities."

Spencer stiffened, his vision locked on the road and the cars that passed by every now and again. After a few moments, he wiped a hand over his forehead and said, "You're really firing me?"

"Oui."

"Well, then Mr. LeRoy, I would like to ask you one last favor?"

"What?"

"Shove a couple crepes and a café au lait up your ass." He slapped the phone shut.

Chapter 11

"Who was that?" Calleigh asked, as Spencer sat back down at the table.

"A very unpleasant telemarketer," he said dazedly, taking off his sunglasses and rubbing the lenses with his shirt sleeve.

"You were on the phone with them a while," she noted.

"They were selling pirated Billy Idol albums. I tried to barter for them with my old lawnmower. Things got tense."

Calleigh exhaled but smiled. "Well, I ordered you a cowboy burger. Figured you wouldn't mind the barbeque sauce and bacon…"

He kept rubbing at his sunglasses. "Great."

"You sure you're okay?"

"Yeah." He folded them and hooked them on his shirt collar.

Their meal came in the next few minutes. They thanked the staff, walked outside, and sat on the curb. Calleigh dug into her food quickly, eating half her burger before Spencer had even taken a bite of his own. He stared at it for the longest time, sipping at his cola and thinking about the conversation with LeRoy. That case had been the biggest case he'd worked in a long time. LeRoy was a known figure in the culinary world and his law firm had practically bent over backward to accommodate him.

His choice of words would be less than okay with the partners at the firm. They hadn't been fans of him taking the trip in the first place, only agreeing because of health reasons and because of his paralegal's familiarity with the case. This would just affirm his growing unhappiness toward the job in their eyes. He doubted he'd have a job to come back to in another week.

"The barbeque sauce too much for you?"

He looked up. "What?"

"You've taken one bite of that burger in the last ten minutes," Calleigh said, scoffing. "Are you sure you're feeling okay?"

"I'm fine. I was just...thinking."

"Think and eat," she said. Her tone suggested more care than command and he suddenly realized that they still had to figure out a way of getting out of this town.

He took a bite of the burger. The taste seemed to set his senses on fire, revitalizing him and kicking the memory of LeRoy into the background. "Hopefully that mechanic can find a new alternator for your car."

Calleigh shrugged, crunching into an onion ring. After a few chews she said, "It's an old model. Sure, it would be great if we could but, honestly? I don't have such high hopes for Ida."

Spencer's eyebrows shot up. "Ida?"

"It's the car's name."

"As in Ida Rosenthal? The bra lady?"

Calleigh stopped eating and looked at him, her face void of

expression. "Yes. Because every time I look at my car I think, "Mmm…supportive in times of severe gravity.""

Spencer chuckled. "Hey, you named your dog Newton. I thought you had a theme going."

She shook her head. "Ida Lupino, genius."

"Your car? Gorgeous Hollywood actress? Not seeing the connection."

"When I got that car, I was dating someone with a Humphrey Bogart fascination. We'd just seen <u>High Sierra,</u> and we were a little drunk…"

"Imagine that."

"Anyway, he named my car Ida and I named his Humphrey and the name just stuck."

"And the guy that had the Bogart obsession? Where did he end up?"

She gave a faint smile and tilted her head back to look at the clouds. "Who knows."

Spencer nodded, letting the comment roll across his mind as he took another swig of his cola .

*

Spending the day in the automotive office felt like being inside a terrarium again for Spencer. *At least it doesn't have prom banners on the walls,* he thought gazing around. The only plant in view was a sickly looking cactus that had begun to deflate in the center, the dirt around it overwatered. He stared out the window at the sky as the sun

144

continued to beat its relentless heat on the dented hoods, dinged doors, and disassembled car frames in the lot out front.

The mechanic appeared at around five o'clock wiping his brow and announced in a dejected tone similar to Droopy Dog that they didn't get a call back from any of their usual salvage yards but that they would try again tomorrow. He told them about a motel down the road where they could stay and in as graceless a manner as any, told them he was closing up shop for the evening. Grabbing their luggage, Spencer and Calleigh walked down the block to the Fresh Stop motel.

"You think we should tell them that they're only one letter away from being a brand of cat litter?" Spencer whispered to Calleigh as he grabbed them a room. She cracked a smile but her eyes were far away, no doubt distracted by financial woes.

Once they got up to the room, Calleigh told Spencer she would take Newton for a walk and disappeared out the open door. He watched her walk down the sidewalk, the corgi waddling happily beside her although her own stride was less carefree and her shoulders stiff.

Not a minute after she'd left, Spencer's phone rang once again. This time he recognized the number. It took him everything he had to press the answer button. "Hello, Chuck,"

"Spencer," the low husky voice said over the line. Chuck Water-Green was a partner at the practice where Spencer worked. He sounded like Jimmy Stewart after he'd smoked seventy packs of cigarettes, coughing every now and again but always pronouncing the

145

's' sounds as 'sh'. "I assume you know why I'm calling you."

Spencer nodded although he knew Chuck couldn't see it. "He's a lunatic, Chuck."

"You and I both know that," Chuck said, "But LeRoy is also a high profile client, one that this firm needs."

"We don't."

Chuck coughed. "Excuse me?"

"We don't need parasites like him," Spencer clarified. "We don't need to represent people who take advantage of the hard work that other people do for them. We shouldn't."

"That's not your call to make."

Spencer cleared his throat. "I think I just made it."

"By telling him to shove some crepes up his ass?" Chuck yelled.

Spencer put a hand on his forehead.

"Jesus, Spencer. Hell, I bet there are dozens of people who want to say that to him every day. You know why they don't?"

"Because they're afraid to."

"Because it wouldn't do any good," Chuck said. "Why did you say it, Spencer?"

"I just told you why."

Chuck was silent a moment and Spencer knew he was pursing his lips like he always did when he knew someone was lying. "I know things have been rough for you. I do. The accident, the divorce—"

"Don't beat around the bush," Spencer said, tiredly. "Just tell

146

me."

Chuck coughed again. "I think you need a change, a big change; something this place can't offer you anymore."

Spencer inhaled. "Say it."

"We have to let you go."

The words seemed to pass through him like light through a colored filter. What ordinarily would have ripped the last shreds of dignity from him instead felt like a giant weight suddenly being lifted from his shoulders. "Thanks, Chuck," he finally said.

"You can clean out your office when you get back."

If I come back. "Sure," he answered instead.

The line went dead.

He sat on the end of his bed and stared out the open door at the sky as it grew steadily darker. After a few minutes, he turned back to the nightstand and opened the drawer, found a phone book inside, and flipped to the yellow pages.

*

Six o'clock wound around. Calleigh had just fed Newton and was just punching in the number to order takeout from a restaurant up the road.

"Order it for pick-up," Spencer told her, digging through his backpack.

She glanced over her shoulder at him. "How? We don't have a car."

As if on cue, a silver Nissan Versa pulled into the parking spot in front of their room and honked once. Spencer sprung up from the bed and went outside to greet the driver. After signing a few forms, and going over the exterior of the car with the man, Spencer collected the keys from him and walked back inside to Calleigh.

She stared at him. "What's that?"

"It's a rhinoceros with wheels," he laughed. "What do you mean? It's our ticket out of here."

The shock didn't vanish from her face. "Did you buy it?"

"Calleigh, the car costs fourteen thousand dollars. I didn't buy it in twenty minutes over the telephone. It's a rental."

"How much did it cost?"

"Less than a new alternator."

Calleigh stood up from the bed and crossed her arms. "You didn't have to…"

"How else were we going to make it to this conference on time?" he asked. "I'll be right back. I've got to give this guy a ride back to the car lot. Then we can pick up our dinner to go."

"Spence…"

"We'll talk later, okay?"

She didn't answer and that was all he needed as confirmation that he'd made the right choice. Moving over to the car, he climbed in and drove the car out of the lot, watching Calleigh's confusion morph into a smile in the rearview mirror.

*

After picking up their food, they collected a refund from the hotel for the room, piled their bags and Newton into the car and set off down the road once more. Spencer took the wheel, letting Calleigh eat her chicken alfredo. Each pleasant slurp and groan made him realize how empty his stomach was. He'd only taken a few bites of his lunch before that uneasy feeling had come back and made him not hungry. He was regretting not finishing that burger now.

Painted in orange and purple watercolor streaks, the sky finally deepened into blackness. Headlights lit up the highway around them like glowing orbs in the summer heat, focusing Spencer's attention on the road. The newer Nissan was a much smoother ride than Calleigh's car had been and the air conditioning didn't smell like dog hair, much to his relief.

Newton yawned in the backseat, and turned around several times before settling down in a little ball, his chin resting on the seat. Calleigh put an arm behind her head and took a deep breath. Once they had passed out of the city, the countryside opened up all around them. The last greens in the fields faded beneath the paling colors in the sky, slowly eaten by shadows. Little trees lined the sides of the road in small batches like fingers reaching up from the earth to take hold of the highway.

Hours passed in this dark flat world, silence encompassing the car. He kept his eyes on the road, unsure if Calleigh was awake or asleep. When all traces of light had vanished from the horizon, it was the white dotted lines he stared at. They still had countless miles to travel in the next two days in order to make it to Oregon on time.

There was a very real possibility that they'd be driving all night long. The car snafu had cost them precious time and after wasting time the day before, they were practically a full day behind schedule.

Once out of Iowa and into Nebraska, they almost immediately ended up in Omaha, continuing to follow interstate 80. The night traffic was nauseating but Spencer felt a strange new calm fusing with his mind. Something about driving at night eased his discomfort behind the wheel. A semi-truck pulled up next to them, its bestial rumbling breaking him out of his calm only for a few moments before it was caught in a long line. Spencer pressed on the gas pedal and left the truck far behind in the lights of the city as they once again plunged into the darkness of the country.

Out here, the thoughts of home caught up to him quicker. He was going to have to look for a new job when he got back. And his money situation, while it would be okay for now, was going to begin dwindling faster than he'd like. He had car bills to pay when he got back, utilities, rent, and a whole host of other things on top of paying for food. *A month or two... tops,* he figured, scratching the back of his neck. He'd be in trouble if he didn't find a job by then. Even if he found one, he'd be taking a pay cut. The office he'd worked for was literally the best one in Maine. No one else would have the same benefits and pay-grade.

I'm looking at a change in lifestyle here; a big change.

As if on cue, Calleigh suddenly asked, "How much did the car cost to rent?"

He tore his eyes away from the dotted lines. "What does it matter?"

"I want to know so that I can reimburse you when this trip is over."

"You don't have to."

She sat up a little in her seat. "I want to."

"Just buy me some chocolate at the next rest stop and we'll be even."

"If this is your way of apologizing for what happened yesterday, you really don't need to—"

"Can't I just do something nice without you cross-examining me?"

She scoffed. "I just want to know why you won't take my money."

He shivered. The night air had cooled down a lot since they started driving. He pushed a button on the center dash, turning off the AC. "You're still going to have to pay for a new alternator, don't forget."

"Can I at least pay for half of the rental cost?"

Spencer glanced at her. "Can I just do this for you as a gift?"

"I don't like owing people."

Stubborn as a mule, he mused. "You don't owe me anything."

She quieted. For moments he thought he'd actually won. Then she said, "Just let me pay you back for half of it."

"My god, you're like the unthankful child at Christmas who

gets a doll but rejects it because she wants world peace instead."

"I never said I was unthankful. I just said I don't like owing anyone…"

"Why can't you just accept it?" he shouted.

Calleigh stared at him, wide-eyed.

"Why can't you just let me do it out of the goodness of my damned heart?"

She cleared her throat. "Well, now that you've put it so nicely…"

Silence ate up the space between him. He returned his eyes to the road, shaking his head. "I'm sorry."

"You've been weird ever since that phone call this afternoon. What's going on with you?"

"I just…"

"Pull over up here."

"You're not going to kick me out again, are you?"

Her expression softened. "Just pull over up here."

He negotiated the Versa to the side of the highway and cut the engine. Cars and trucks zoomed by them, each time shaking the car a little bit. Newton had woken in the back seat and lay there, his large brown eyes staring at Spencer in the rearview mirror. He whined.

"What happened?" Calleigh asked him again.

"I got into it with my client on the phone. He fired me."

"He sounds like he was an asshole anway," Calleigh said, rolling her eyes. "There are going to be other clients you can help…"

152

"I got laid off."

Her smirk slid off her face. "What?"

"My boss called me while you were walking the dog. He sacked me."

"Because you and your client had a disagreement? Seems pretty unworthy to me."

"I may have told him to shove some French food up his ass."

"Oh." She nodded. "Well then, yeah. That would do it."

"Yeah."

Newton stood up and climbed through the space between their seats, settling in Calleigh's lap. She rubbed his head, her eyes never leaving Spencer. "Why did you do it?"

"I guess I didn't care anymore."

"Spencer, when we first met, you used your job as an excuse to not come on this trip with me. Obviously it mattered enough then."

He rubbed his hands through his hair. "I mean I didn't care about the life I have. In those few moments on the phone earlier today, I realized that I really didn't care what I had to go back to because none of it was important. The Lexus, the apartment, the stupid job… none of it has any meaning to me anymore."

Calleigh gave him an uneasy look. "When you say "you don't care about the life you have", you don't mean—"

He gave her a stern look. "I'm not suicidal, Calleigh."

She exhaled. "Good."

"I'm just saying that things in my life have changed…but I

haven't. And it's not working like this."

"You mean your divorce, right."

He stared at the road ahead of the car, the grass in the fields swishing back and forth in the breeze just beyond the headlights. "Yeah."

Newton pushed his muzzle into Calleigh's armpit, whining for attention. She rubbed his ear.

"Our marriage was solid. I thought it was solid," he said. "Married for thirteen years and suddenly, one accident changes it all."

"A car accident?" Calleigh guessed.

He nodded. "It was raining. I was late for work. I'd pulled up to an intersection with a light. I went to grab something that had fallen on the passenger side floor and rolled under the seat. When I looked up the light was yellow. I had missed the green light and I didn't want to have to wait through another red light so I pulled out. A mac truck across from me apparently had the same idea as me and tried to turn left."

The image of seeing the truck's grill so close flashed in his mind. He closed his eyes and inhaled. The screech of metal on metal pierced his ears in the memory, making him cringe. He felt a hand on his. He opened his eyes to see Calleigh's palm resting on the back of his hand.

She nodded at him to continue.

"I was in the hospital for weeks. Broke my left arm in a couple places, dislocated my shoulder, cracked a few ribs, had a hell of a concussion..."

"Sounds like you got off lucky," Calleigh said, shaking her head. "You could have easily died."

"I know. Believe me, I know."

"When did things start going downhill?"

He straightened in his seat and inhaled deeply. "After the first panic attack. Lydia wanted me to stay home from work more. She didn't want me driving as much. But, she was transitioning jobs at that point and there wasn't any other income aside from what I was bringing in. I had to work. She didn't even like the idea of a vacation, because she was worried about me having an episode somewhere away from home. Fighting with her became so exhausting."

"She was probably just scared for you."

"I know she was." He rubbed his eyes. "But I was angry about it. Instead of feeling like I had her support, I felt like she was treating me as an invalid. It got annoying. And on top of it all, she wanted to talk about the accident. I didn't. We started fighting and never stopped."

Calleigh looked down at Newton, but didn't say anything.

"The worst of it all is that I know it's my own damn fault. I know that if I'd just talked about it once with her, everything might have turned out differently. If I hadn't been so afraid, I could have saved us."

"It takes two to fight, Spencer. We both know that."

He put his head in his hands. "I hate it. I hate going home to the empty house and knowing that I'd asked for it."

"Spencer, look at me," Calleigh said.

He turned his head.

"What happened between you and your ex-wife was terrible. Every time two people who love one another separate, it's terrible in its own way," her voice cracked. "You have to acknowledge that what you two had together was beautiful at one time. Those memories are the ones worth keeping. Remember those, mourn them, and then look to the future."

Spencer felt the tears welling up in his eyes and looked down at the seat, sighing. "I have no idea what I'm going to do now."

"Sometimes, it takes a bit of wandering to discover where to go next," she said. "For now though, let's go to this conference. After that, you can decide where you need to go."

He closed his eyes, forcing the tears back. "Okay."

Calleigh rubbed his shoulder in little circular motions as he let all of the thoughts about Lydia subside into the background. The tension in his body gave way the longer they sat there in silence and after a minute, he opened his eyes, and wiped them with the sleeve of his shirt.

"Wow," he said, sniffling. "You'd make a hell of a therapist."

She smiled. "Got a minor in psychology."

"Why am I not surprised?" he chuckled. He turned over the Nissan's engine and it purred alive in moments.

"Want me to take the wheel?" she asked.

"I'm good. I'm okay." He checked his watch. "So we still have...how long to drive?"

"Well, we still have over a thousand miles to drive through the rest of Nebraska, Wyoming, Utah, Idaho, and then some of Oregon. I'd say about twenty-four hours on the road."

Spencer nodded. "It's going to be a long night."

"Hey, if we make it to Cheyenne by tomorrow morning, I'll be happy."

"Okay then." Spencer shifted the car into drive and waited for the traffic to clear before pulling back out onto the highway.

"Are you sure you don't want me to drive?" she asked again.

"I'll be fine until about one or so. You get to drive the early morning shift while I sleep."

She glared. "I should have just let you self-destruct."

"But then you'd have probably been driving the entire thing yourself."

Calleigh pointed a finger at him. "I'll have dark plans for you."

"Better get some shut eye, cupcake. Your shift will be here before you know it."

She shook her head, smirking as she hefted Newton into the back and reclined her seat.

Spencer looked up at the stars spread across the navy sky, letting them be his map as he began the long journey through the night.

Chapter 12

The sound of rain pattering on the roof of the car awoke Spencer from his sleep. He began to sit up but groaned and stayed where he was. The headache that had formed during the night of driving hadn't gone away like he'd hoped it would. The long night and his discussion with Calleigh had wound him up. His stomach had begun a chorus of growling shortly after he resumed driving. It had gotten so loud that Calleigh eventually tossed a granola bar at him and told him if he didn't eat it, she'd force feed it to him.

Still, it was only a granola bar. His stomach had panged with hunger the rest of the night. But at some point, it hadn't mattered. It was unconsciousness that was trying to pull him down. The long days they'd spent in the car had completely shattered his normal sleep schedule. He found that whenever they rolled into a place for the night, he was out cold within ten minutes of hitting the pillow. It hadn't bothered him then. It did now.

He knew he could just pull off the side of the road, turn off the car, and let sleep's tangles eventually overtake him. Guilt got the better of him. All he could think of was how much time they'd lost the day before because of their little argument, how much time they'd lost because of Calleigh's decrepit car… He didn't want to waste any more of it. He knew it was smarter to just pull over, and knew that if she had any idea how tired he was, she'd probably punch him. None of it persuaded him otherwise.

Time drug as the miles went by. The endless blur of those dotted lines in the headlights made him feel as if he was looking through a warped mirror at the world. He began seeing shapes in the fields of things that didn't belong, trees that pulled up their own roots and seemed to be running alongside them, keeping pace with the car. As his mind battled with trying to determine whether they were real or not, he found himself drifting in the lane. The car suddenly vibrated as the tires hit the rumble strip and the high-pitched whine immediately woke Calleigh and Newton.

"What the hell's going on?" she'd said, bolting up in her seat, as he corrected the car back onto the asphalt.

"Squirrel," he'd answered.

She'd made him pull over and switch places with her.

He barely remembered Calleigh taking his seat behind the wheel. Now, he gazed over at her. Her eyes were red and her face in that expressionless state somewhere between fatigue and inattention.

She needs a break, he thought. He was having a hard enough time as it was keeping his eyes open, though, and knew he wouldn't last long behind the wheel. *Maybe we can just take an hour to rest...* As soon as the words were out of his mouth, he knew it would never happen. They'd all sleep through the day without some kind of a reminder to wake them up.

"How'd you sleep?" she asked as if on cue.

"Like a crack addict watching National Geographic."

"Yeah, you mentioned something about the trees "running really fast"," she scoffed.

"I didn't mention anything about one with a banjo, did I?"

She shook her head. "Though now I'm intrigued."

He flopped his head toward the passenger side window and sighed. "The less you know, the better."

In what felt like very little time at all, the sky had turned into an ethereal tropical blue edged by storm clouds. It was the kind of blue that almost never existed in nature, the kind of blue that was reserved for exotic locales, places where the sun could brightly ignite the sea and play with the eyes. It didn't seem as though it existed here. For a long time, Spencer wondered if he was dreaming again. There was a weight missing from his shoulders, one that had made it so hard to think the day before.

The sadness would never fully lift, he understood. There was always going to be a little hole inside him from letting Lydia leave, a hole that would make it more than difficult for him to feel complete. But he also knew that acknowledging this out loud had done something to him. It had lessened those gut-twisting worries he'd been clenching for years. It was hard to see how things could change. But somehow, staring into the uniquely colored sky, he was sure he was going to be okay. He didn't have to make any decisions right now. That was all that mattered.

"We're about fifteen hours away," Calleigh announced as they pulled into a tiny filling station to refill the tank.

The convenience store was small and looked as though it had been converted out of an old shed. Spencer eyed the weathered wood, rusty nails, and timeworn outer walls, displaying old banners for colas and cigarettes. "Looks like this thing barely survived the Dust Bowl," he said more to himself than to Calleigh as she lifted the hose and flipped the metal lever on the side of the pump. He hadn't seen a gas tank like that in over fifteen years.

"Why don't you go inside and grab us something to eat," Calleigh called, not hearing him.

Inside the convenience store was like stepping into another world. The Scissor Sisters played low over a radio behind the counter. An older man with a long braid of grey hair running down the back of his leather vest sat there. He leaned back in his old desk chair, boots propped on the counter, reading a dog-earred paperback copy of Hemingway's The Old Man and The Sea.

Willie Nelson called. He wants his ponytail back.

The man's eyes flicked up to meet him, his gaze wary.

"Hi."

The man nodded but didn't say anything.

Spencer didn't push it. He wandered to the back of the store, grabbed two bottles of water from the fridge and browsed the aisles for something breakfast like. He couldn't find anything save for a couple of Twinkies. He frowned. Calleigh wouldn't be pleased. But then

161

again, what had she expected when she'd pulled up to this place? It didn't exactly inspire visions of a bakery with warm muffins and boiling coffee. The thought nearly carried him away. He couldn't wait until he had some coffee.

He dropped everything on the counter in front of the man who begrudgingly put his book aside and began ringing up the various items.

"You paying for gas, too?"

"Yeah. Thirty bucks." Spencer's eyes fell on the book again. "That's a great book."

"I don't like Hemingway," the man grumbled.

"Then why are you reading it?"

"Because it's the only book I've got here until Marcie shows up to collect the damn recyclables."

Spencer's eyebrows shot up as he fished his credit card out of his wallet and handed it over the counter.

The man stared at him and pointed to a sign covertly hidden amongst the various cigarette lighters, postcards, lottery tickets, and sixties paraphernalia. Cash only.

Spencer sighed as he slipped the credit card back and slid a few bills out. "Does she bring you a new book every week?"

"She brings me what she thinks I should read. Tries to get me to read things that will make me think about how alone I am."

Spencer's hand froze in the air as he passed the bill over.

The man slid the money out of his hand and popped out the

162

register drawer, plucking out the change. "Like I need a reminder. It's just like a woman to do that though."

Spencer barely felt the change plunk into his hand. *I don't want to be like you.*

"Thanks," he said under his breath, gathering everything and walking out to the car.

Calleigh was just placing the gas hose back against the tank as he rounded to take his place behind the wheel. "Twinkies? Really?"

"Unless you were in the mood for beef jerky and salted peanuts, you'll respect my decision," he said, letting the items spill over the passenger seat. Newton lunged up to investigate the snacks. Spencer pushed him back.

Calleigh started toward the store. "I'll just pay for the gas and then—"

"It's already done. We're set to go."

She eyed him. "Really? I was supposed to get this one."

"I spared you," was all he said before shutting the door. Moments later, Calleigh opened the passenger side door and climbed in, moving the snacks into her lap. As they pulled out of the gas station, she opened a package of the Twinkies and handed one to Spencer. "What did you spare me from?"

"Just trust me." He took a big bite of the Twinkie.

"Okay," she said hesitantly.

The car sped off down the road into the flat landscape, accentuated by the now grey sky.

*

Spencer was grateful when they stopped at a roadside diner store and picked up some food to go nearly an hour later. All the Twinkie had managed to do was make him feel sick and Calleigh didn't look much better after wolfing hers down.

After walking Newton around the building a few times, they climbed back in the car and spent the next several hours driving. The car was perfumed with the rich aroma of roasted potatoes and bacon which had permeated that "new car smell" all too quickly.

By mid-afternoon, they were in Utah and had successfully found their way around Salt Lake City without having to go through it on Rt. 84. They decided to take a break for lunch at a diner. However, when Spencer looked around, all he saw in the parking lot were motorcycles. "I'm pretty sure this is a biker bar," he said to Calleigh as her seat belt slithered off her lap.

"That sign said "Diner"."

"Camouflage."

"Spence—"

"Why don't we just get it to go and get back in the car? We've still got a lot of driving to do."

"We've cleared nearly twelve hours of driving since last night." She sighed. "Please. Let's just sit down and get something to eat. I'm starving and I need to be out of the car for a little bit."

"Sure, I could use a break from all that sitting," Spencer said, his tone biting as he opened his door. "Let's go sit some more."

As he climbed out of the door, his legs tingled and almost seemed to go numb. He held onto the car door, feeling a cramp suddenly shoot up his thigh. "Aw, shit."

Calleigh was cringing on the other side of the car, very slowly working her way around the front toward him. "I think my leg muscles have atrophied," she said.

"I think mine are just goo now," he answered, feeling the pain race up his back. Both of them hobbled toward the door of the diner and went inside.

Spencer was aware of a hustle and bustle that was common for a place like this roadside diner in mid-afternoon, especially with all of the bikes parked outside. Except that the moment the bell chimed when they walked in, it had come to a dead halt. All the eyes in the diner, mostly from gritty bikers donned in leather and dark sunglasses despite the dim atmosphere of the place, were all centered right on them. The conversation had petered out so that just the Elvis tune on the radio could be heard, lending an eeriness to the already unwelcoming atmosphere.

Calleigh leaned toward Spencer. "Do I have something in my teeth?"

"You'd think we were walking in here naked or something."

A waitress appeared from the kitchen, a larger woman with sparkling blue eyes and a wide grin. "How are you folks doing today?"

"Peachy," Spencer said, unable to take his eyes off of the still staring patrons.

165

"We don't get too many tourists in here. Usually the outside of the building scares them off."

He elbowed Calleigh. "Told you."

"Would you like a table?"

Before Spencer could say no, Calleigh accepted and she guided them to their seat passing by all of the gawking eyes. They took a booth at the far back of the establishment. Calleigh sat with her back to the rest of the diners while Spencer sat facing them, preferring to know exactly what they were up to. The men in the booth behind them were still watching, their glasses of beer suspended in midair.

"Hi!" Spencer finally said.

They both turned back to their conversation, grumbling.

Calleigh stared at him for a time. Then he realized how tight his shoulders were.

"Your parents didn't leave you in a biker bar, too, did they?"

"Very funny."

"Look, we won't be here for very long."

"Good," he said, feeling another gaze on him. Another older biker was watching him from one of the barstools across the way. He didn't look away, his eyes narrowing into slits. "Every time I look up, I feel like Steven Seagal is glaring at me."

"You know, I think I understand the hostility," Calleigh said, perusing the menu.

"Good because I don't."

"It's a territorial thing."

"Really?"

"This is their space where they can be accepted. We're outsiders invading it. We don't fit into their social group."

He chuckled. "Why do I feel like I'm watching National Geographic again?"

The waitress reappeared and took their order. The diner quieted once again for this momentous event, and Spencer suddenly felt as if he was standing on stage proclaiming his dietary habits for all to hear. When the waitress scuttled back to the kitchen, he leaned over the table and said, "How much longer until we're there?"

"Another nine to ten hours, tops. We can be there on time for the registration tomorrow if we get to Nampa tonight."

"In Idaho?"

She took a sip of the lemonade that the waitress had dropped off. "I da ho. Do you ho?"

Spencer shook his head but found himself smiling at the joke. "That was bad."

"Hey, a full night and most of a day spent in the car, you can't blame me if some of my brain cells melted in there."

The food came pretty quickly, much to Spencer's surprise. Talking with Calleigh seemed to make the time go by so much faster and he was welcome for that feeling. Anything to take his mind off of the unsettling atmosphere and his thoughts of the night before was great. Soon enough, he had completely tuned out their surroundings, lost in a story about Calleigh's first night back at college for her master's degree.

"God, it was horrible!" she said, laughing. "I spent the night rolling around, listening to someone practicing their classical violin across the hall, a male cheerleader shouting his cheers in the room on my right, and a kid playing World of Warcraft in the room on my left all night long."

Spencer laughed and took a sip of his beer. "Why didn't you get an apartment?"

"I was working nights as a clerk at a gas station and already had a bunch of money to pay in loans. I couldn't afford it. Though now I wish I'd just done it anyway." She wiped her mouth with a napkin and put it down on the table. "I'll be right back."

"Sure."

She stood and walked off toward the bathroom, vanishing around the corner.

He finished off his beer and ate a French fry from the plate. He began to think about how little time they had left until they actually got there, until they were standing in some forest out in the middle of Oregon, listening to workshops on who knew what. They would only be there for a couple days or so and then would have to begin the drive back. That would be another week of driving though, another week to figure out what he really wanted to do. He looked down at his lap. *I'm fifty and I feel like I'm starting all over again.* The thrill of the revelation was instantly followed by fear. *Just don't screw it up this time.*

"Son of a bitch!"

His head shot up. Calleigh's voice had rung out from somewhere around the corner. He stood and found his way down the hall to the bathrooms. He spotted her instantly. Their server was holding Calleigh back as she strained against her. Her eyes were on fire with rage, one he'd never seen an equal of until that moment. Her hands were clenched into fists.

A bald man with a scruffy beard and a blue bandana tied at his neck was smirking at her from his seat at the bar, smooching at her. The others sitting near him had distanced themselves from him, disapproval in their faces.

Spencer stalked toward Calleigh, his blood already igniting with fury as his thoughts raced ahead of him. "Let her go," he told the waitress who obliged but kept herself rooted between Calleigh and the man. "What's going on?"

Calleigh pointed over the waitress's shoulder at the man. "This douchebag just slapped my ass," she said with a shaking voice.

The man shrugged. "I couldn't help it. It was begging for a little attention."

The waitress rolled her eyes. "Dean has trouble keeping his hands to himself."

"You friggin' jerk," Calleigh spat over the waitress's shoulder.

Spencer stepped in front of her. "Why don't you just apologize to the lady?"

Dean gave him a once over. "Who are you; her sugar daddy?"

169

Spencer rolled his eyes. "No, I'm actually her lawyer."

Dean stood, his figure towering over Spencer's. "Oh, so now you're going to sue me? Is that it?"

"I imagine sexual harassment is a pretty laudable claim," Spencer said, not taking his eyes away from Dean's.

The waitress turned to him and gave him a stern look. "Knock it off, Dean. I really don't want to have to call the cops two days in a row."

Dean stepped into Spencer's face. The stench of cigarettes wafted over him and it took everything he had not to squint or cough.

"She came out of that bathroom just asking for it. You could see it in her eyes, the way she swung those hips…"

"I did not *swing* my hips!" Calleigh snarled.

Dean ignored her. "You could just see she wanted some attention…from a man. Not from some puke like you."

The hair on Spencer's arms stood on end. "Yeah, you're a regular Adonis."

Dean growled.

"You must really impress the ladies with that aftershave. What is it? Eau de Nicotine?"

"You better watch it, pal, before I—"

"And that goatee?" Spencer continued, "Looks like something I saw shoveled off the road a few days ago."

Before Spencer knew what was happening, Dean's fist smashed into his face. He went down much faster than he wanted, clipping one of the tables behind him with his elbow.

"Holy shit!" Calleigh yelled.

Spencer's left eye felt as though it was on fire. All he could see was a spot that changed from black to neon green every few seconds. He put a hand to it blocking half of his view of the world.

"Dean! That's enough! Get out before I call the cops," the waitress shouted.

Dean rumbled with pride as he stomped off toward the door.

"Oh my god, Spencer!" Calleigh said, crouching next to him.

"I'm fine," he said, sitting up and looking at the waitress. "Any chance we could get some ice to go?"

Chapter 13

"Feeling any better?" Calleigh asked.

Spencer slowly turned to look toward her from the passenger seat of the Nissan, pulling the sandwich bag of mostly melted ice from his eye. "It still feels like there's a power drill trying to get through my head."

She cringed as she glanced at him. "It's already bruising."

He turned back to the window. In the side-view mirror, he could see a shiny purple ring swelling underneath his left eye. "Great."

Calleigh chuckled. "Eau de Nicotine?"

"Usually I'm better with my comebacks."

"I thought it was pretty funny."

He sighed. "Yeah, just about as funny as when he knocked me flat."

Newton crawled through the seat, until his upper half rested on Spencer's lap. He laid his hand on the dog's head and Newton's tail wagged excitedly.

She cleared her throat. "By the way…uh…thanks."

"No problem. He was a jackass," he said although his mind was reeling. Did she actually just thank him? He could tell by the way she shifted her eyes away that she didn't want to sit on the subject or acknowledge that she'd once again been helped. He pressed the squishy damp sandwich bag over his face again and closed his eyes.

Time seemed to pass in flickers of light. The rain would come and go in micro showers, the sun making its slow arc behind the soft shimmering grey clouds. By nighttime, the storm had drifted off. Stars shone across the navy sky like reflections on the water. They reminded Spencer of Maine. When he and Lydia had found their first place together, they bought what the locals referred to as a "camp". It was a tiny lodge on a lake out in the backwoods, far from the sounds of traffic, summer tourists, and, unfortunately, indoor plumbing. While living there, it was hard to imagine how it could have been tranquil, what with finding bats hanging from the curtains in the mornings, laundry blowing up into the trees from the wind, and the generator keeling over every time they tried to make toast and boil coffee at the same time.

Hindsight made it seem awful. It wasn't though. They were, as he so eloquently put it once, "roughing it" out in the Maine woods for the first five years of their lives. It was before they had settled into their careers and into their marriage. Things were still spontaneous and much like the dock spiders that occasionally leapt out of swimming trunks left to dry in the sun, one never knew exactly what was going to happen from day to day.

He missed that naivety, that blissful ignorance about the future.

Calleigh pulled the car off the highway and through a small town, the lone light from a flickering neon bar sign that they soon left behind.

She eventually pulled the car over to the side of the road just alongside a rocky expanse, the only vegetation short dry grass and the occasional smear of red from a desert paintbrush. Jagged mountainsides carved a crooked line on the horizon to their immediate right and further off on their left, creating a natural bowl around them.

When Calleigh found them a bare spot, he turned on lanterns for a perimeter and pitched the tent, while she took Newton to relieve his poor dog bladder. Spencer had already fired up the camp stove by the time she returned.

"What'll it be tonight?" he asked, pulling out a couple bags of freeze-dried food. "Chilean Sea Bass with mashed potato or Chicken a la King?"

"Chicken," she said without a moment's hesitation.

"Should I be worried about the fish?"

"Not unless you enjoy eating something that tastes like wet paper."

"I'm a lawyer. I eat paper for breakfast."

She rolled her eyes at him as she turned around and hiked back up to the road to get something from the car.

He screwed the tiny camp stove apparatus to the can of fuel and grabbed the thermos from nearby to fill up the container. When he looked up, a grin curled onto his face.

Calleigh returned from the car, holding a gleaming full bottle of scotch.

"Where on Earth did you get that?"

She sat down in a nylon chair next to him and plunked the bottle down into the dusty earth. "You remember that gas station in Nebraska?"

"Which one?"

Her face scrunched up as she tried to remember. "Kearney?"

"The one with that guy standing in the middle of the McDonald's parking lot next door who couldn't remember the alphabet?"

Calleigh scraped at the plastic around the screw top with a fingernail. "He got some of the letters right."

"From what I remember, the end went something like, "Now I know my STD's, next time won't you sleep with me?""

She put a fist to her heart. "He made it his own."

"Let me know when it tops the charts."

Calleigh peeled away the rest of the plastic and tossed it into a bag nearby. "Anyway, there was also a little distillery on the opposite side of the gas station. I happened to find this beauty hiding in the back away from the more innocuous brands of booze."

She unscrewed the top and took a deep breath, sighing. "Mmm."

The mellow sweet scent wafted toward Spencer. It had been years since he'd had scotch, the last time being at an office Christmas party where one of the partners, Chuck, had brought it in with the misconception they would savor its aroma and swirl it around in a glass like seasoned tasters. The bottle hadn't lasted an hour.

Calleigh held the bottle aloft, where they both stared at its seductive amber splendor against the starlight. Newton stared up at it from his spot across from them, his head slightly cocked and large ears perked.

Calleigh cleared her throat. "We have driven almost the entire length of the United States in the last five days and tomorrow, we will finally reach our destination. I would like to toast our last night on the road."

"To all of the pointless arguments, ridiculous situations, and absurd people we've met," Spencer added. "May we never have anything to do with any of you again."

"Especially that guy in the McDonald's parking lot," Calleigh muttered before lifting the scotch to her lips and taking a swig.

He accepted the bottle from her as she stood up and promptly lost her balance, falling back down into the chair. "You've never had scotch before, have you?" he asked.

"I've always wanted to try it."

"You do realize this is some pretty powerful stuff, right?"

"That's why I got it," she said, finally standing up.

"You want to spend the last night before the conference starts getting drunk?"

"Oh, come on, Spence!" Calleigh called, clipping Newton to his leash and running off into the bristling grass with Newton's chunky form trying to keep up. "Cut loose! Have fun! You're starting over, aren't you?"

He cocked his head. *Guess I am.* He took a long pull from the bottle. Within a few minutes, the ground beneath him seemed to tip to one side. This was definitely not Chuck's fine single malt whiskey. He turned the bottle around to read the contents. "Cask strength! This scotch is nearly 60 proof!"

"Again, that's why I got it!" Calleigh shouted back to him, her form melding with the darkness so that just her white blouse stood out like a bodiless apparition.

He shook his head. *We'll be lucky if we can stand in the morning, let alone drive from here to Oregon.*

Screw it.

Spencer took another swig from the bottle, enjoying the malted caramel flavor and the hint of smokiness to accompany it. The world began to blend together as if being mixed like paint on a small palette. *May some higher power make sure I don't do something stupid.*

*

Spencer ran across the dry grass after Calleigh's fleeting form. Her giggling rippled up into the night, echoing off the cliffsides around them. Newton's shrill barking came from somewhere behind, no doubt frantic in an effort to catch up with the two of them.

He stopped and bent over to try and catch his breath. The scotch was like a hot stone sitting in his stomach, burning up his throat. But the pleasant coziness it provided was the only thing about it that mattered. The camp stove, tent, and sleeping bags had been left far behind in the world of late night and tomorrow morning, a place where they'd eventually stumble once they'd returned from this other plane of euphoria. That world could wait.

When he righted himself, he noticed that Calleigh had scrambled on top of a large boulder and was standing precariously at the top, laughing.

"What are you doing?" he called, starting toward her again.

"This rock is AH-mazing!"

"Yeah, so is Stone Hedge, but you don't go climbing that. Get down from there."

Calleigh posed, a hand on her hip the other combing through her chestnut hair. "Want to know why this rock is so amazing?"

"Because you're standing on it?"

"Because I'm standing on it!"

Spencer stood directly beneath her, staring up and staggered to one side a little. "Get down from there! You're going to fall and crack your head open and then I'll get in trouble."

Calleigh blew a raspberry at him. "You are the safest person I know!"

"You should be wearing a helmet, just in case. Do we have any of those? Helmets?" He stared out across the field toward the car. "I'll go get you one."

"Get up here!" She crouched down and extended a hand to him.

"I just said—"

"Stop being a mommy and get your ass up here."

He grabbed hold of her palm and planted his foot against a small knick in the boulder. She pulled as he jumped. Their hands slipped and he tumbled backward onto the ground.

Calleigh roared with laughter.

Spencer flipped over and propped himself on his knees. "See? Didn't I say this would happen?"

"Well, it doesn't help that your hand's all sweaty," Calleigh chuckled, wiping her hand on her shorts. "I felt like I was trying to pull a jellyfish up here."

"Are you implying that I have no strength?"

She cocked her head. "Well, you *did* fall…"

"Okay, then. Get ready." He backed up a few steps and ran toward the boulder and leapt. His toes caught in the nook in the rock and he launched himself up toward her. She grabbed his hand and pulled him the rest of the way up.

Calleigh nodded. "That was pretty amazing. Very Scott Hamilton of you."

He groaned as he held his leg and he sat down beside her. "It's been about twenty years since I did a triple-lutz, much less jumped like that."

She put an arm around him and leaned her head onto his shoulder. "Felt good, didn't it?"

"Yeah," he said, leaning his head on hers. "But ask me again in the morning. The alcohol makes it hard to feel any pain and I may have dislocated a hip."

"Old man."

They laid back, Spencer's arm cushioning her head and hers cushioning his as they picked out constellations in the sky.

"See those two bright stars there?" he asked.

"Yeah."

"And that string of stars all in a line there that kind of looks like a smile?"

"No. Wait…yes."

He whispered in her ear, "That's the constellation of Regis Philbin."

They both lost control, twin laughter that was so loud it echoed far into the night sky. They listened to it disappear until the silence returned in full force.

He took a deep breath. "Your hair smells really good."

She glanced at him, putting her hand to her heart. "Wow, a compliment. I didn't think you were actually capable of giving those," she joked.

"What? It smells nice. I'm glad you didn't do a PTA shower this morning."

She rolled, landing on top of him as she began to smack him. "Shut up."

He fought off her hands, but was powerless to stop her bending down and kissing him, her lips stopping a long list of ribbing jokes he'd had planned.

Don't do anything stupid. The words suddenly didn't matter. Spencer's impulse got the best of him as he leaned into her kiss, propping himself on one elbow as he put an arm behind her back and pulled her down closer to him. The rest of the night could have gone by fast or slow. He wouldn't have noticed. Just the feeling of her weight on him was enough to finally push away the thoughts still overshadowing him like imminent rainclouds. That feeling of loneliness shattered like Lydia's tiny flower vase had done when he'd finished clearing out the rest of her things. And much like that, he didn't bother to clean up the pieces.

Chapter 14

Spencer coughed and turned over on the sleeping bag, the lingering taste of the scotch bitter in his mouth. He scrunched his face up and pushed himself up from the bag. His head throbbed as though someone had put it between two banging cymbals. His stomach didn't feel much better. He turned over looking for his backpack but realized that it wasn't there. He also realized he wasn't *in* the sleeping bag.

Just as memories about the night before caught up with him, he heard Calleigh scream his name from outside the tent. "Spence!"

He scrambled to his feet, his heart hammering as he unzipped the tent fly and rushed outside.

Calleigh was a few feet away, crouching over something. She was searching her pockets frantically. Her bag was nearby, all of her clothes tossed about haphazardly. As he neared, he felt his breath catch in his throat.

Newton lay in the dirt, his body jerking. At first, he thought perhaps the dog had eaten something he shouldn't have or hurt himself somehow. Then he noticed the white foam at his mouth, the way his eyes had practically rolled up into his head.

"What's going on? What's happening?" he asked, despite already having some idea.

"He's bit! I think a snake bit him and I can't find the car keys. I can't find them!" She spun toward him, tears stinging her eyes. "Help me find them!"

He quickly grabbed his shoes and threw them on. "I'll go look out there. You check through the tent."

She nodded as he raced out into the desert, with his boxers and a white wife-beater on as his only covering. A car passing by on the road honked at him, the headlights illuminating the darkness for only a moment. He got only a few feet before he realized it was no use without a flashlight. He ran back and grabbed one from his bag, dodging Calleigh as she tore at the sleeping bags.

He raced back out into the darkness. His headache banged behind his eyes with every step he took, the bleary flashlight barely giving him a clear view of the grass. Vague memories of running through it last night raced through his mind the further he went. He knew they'd taken off out into the distance a ways, but where exactly? He tried to focus, all the while scanning.

It was pointless, he realized. There were too many shrubs and there was too much ground to cover. The keys could have dropped anywhere and in such dim lighting and under the distress of a hangover, it would be a miracle if he could see it.

Still he persisted. He remembered lying in one spot last night. He remembered Calleigh rolling on top of him. He remembered the kiss. They hadn't been lying on the ground. They were up higher.

He scanned the area ahead of him with the flashlight and

noticed the boulder up against a cliff side. His leg panged with the realization that he'd lunged on top of it the previous night.

There.

Spencer raced toward it, the pounding in his head worsening. He scanned the ground around it, wondering if it dropped out of her pocket when she'd leaned down to help him up. Nothing. He took a few steps back, knowing he needed to climb on top again.

Be Scott Hamilton. Be Scott Hamilton.

He ran toward it and jumped. His foot slid on the slick rock and he dropped, barely landing on his feet. "Come on!" he yelled at himself.

Spencer tried again, this time catching the knick with his foot but not getting enough momentum to jump up.

It had better be up there, he thought trying for the jump again. His foot connected and he launched up, grabbing hold of the top ledge, his fingertips digging into the stone. He grunted as he pulled himself up.

Sweeping the flashlight beam over the rock's surface, he stopped on the silvery glimmer of the keys lying atop a slight crack in the rock. He grabbed them along with a handful of dust and screamed, "Yes!"

Simultaneously across the sky, he heard, "No!"

A heavy stone seemed to thud onto his heart as he stood up straight and stared back across the expanse between him and their camp. There was no movement in the pale glow of the lanterns.

Somehow, he climbed down and ran, his feet tripping over themselves. When he was close enough to hear the sobbing, he slowed and his grip on the keys slackened. They hit the earth with a small jangle. A few steps closer and the whole scene lie before him with a strange shuddering realism. Calleigh was on her knees, leaning over Newton's limp form, hugging him tightly while she sobbed. He couldn't tell if the dog's eyes were open or closed, but he knew he was no longer moving.

Spencer stepped toward her and knelt beside Calleigh. All the words that he knew left him. He put a hand on her shoulder.

She jerked away from him, falling on her side and taking the dog with her. "Don't touch me! Don't touch me…" she cried.

His hand left suspended in the air, Spencer stayed where he was, watching her cradle Newton, a sudden feeling of desertion rising through him. He hated this. He hated being relegated to watch Calleigh suffer alone. The idea struck him like lightning. *You are not that man anymore.*

He crawled over to where she lay and sat behind her. He pulled her upper body into his lap. She didn't fight him. His fingers combed through her hair as he held her and Newton. For hours they stayed that way, not moving. When the sun stung the sky with a tiny red spark, it dashed the shadows to the crooks and crannies in the rocks and revealed the truth to what Calleigh had spent hours in the dark trying to deny.

Spencer finally took Newton from Calleigh and walked back to the boulder. He'd told Calleigh to stay behind but knew that she was following him by the scuffling of her shoes in the dirt. At the boulder, he buried the dog under a pile of rocks. Calleigh stood by sniffling as she held the scruffy green collar, turning it over and over in her hands.

Back at the camp, Spencer started to pack up everything. Calleigh was understandably lost in her own mind and stood a ways away, staring out at the boulder they'd spent hours on the previous night; hours that now seemed like forever ago.

"If you want, I can just drive us to the nearest hotel," Spencer offered, once he'd packed the car. "We can always get to the conference tomorrow."

She shook her head as she turned around, wiping her nose with her hand. "We've spent the last five days busting our asses trying to get to this thing on time. All of that would be in vain if we didn't get there today."

Spencer nodded and tossed her bag over his shoulder. "I'll drive."

"Thanks."

*

Those next few hours spent driving left Spencer time to reflect. Calleigh stared out the passenger window intently, her sunglasses shielding her red tear-streaked eyes. Soon enough, the exhaustion overwhelmed her and she fell asleep.

The whole trip, he'd listened to Calleigh mention new people here and there, while never really bringing them up again during any other story. Those people she'd lived in the dorm with, that old boyfriend that she'd named her car with, even her own parents who she only brought up once to analyze the strength of their marriage. There had been no sort of constant in any of the stories Calleigh had told of her life except for one thing; Newton.

It unfolded in a sort of terrible wretchedness that yanked at Spencer's heart. Those things he'd yelled at her about when they'd fought in Illinois were true; she had no one close save for the dog. She'd let no one else in, for what reason he didn't know. But she'd spent years keeping anyone that could have meant something to her out. And now the only one she had ever truly cared about was gone.

He thought about the chubby little dog, how he'd freaked out about the thunderstorm in Massachusetts, bayed and yipped at the idea of spending the night at the doggy doily inn in New York, assisted in whizzing on the infamous red convertible in Illinois, and tried to eat the fireflies at the camp in Indiana. And for the first time ever, he finally realized why his ex-wife had been so sad about losing her cat all those years ago, why Calleigh was broken about losing Newton now.

He was an amazing animal.

His grip on the wheel tightened as he tried to keep from choking up.

He was a great friend.

*

Relief exploded like a burst of shimmering fireworks over

Spencer when the Nissan crossed from dusty desert in to the rising green mountains of Oregon. While Calleigh shared in his celebration, she was still distanced, her smile quickly regressing into a pained tug at her eyebrows.

Soon after leaving Interstate 84 and merging onto route 26, they found themselves deep within the forest, the sun barely cutting through the trees in mid-afternoon. It reminded Spencer a lot of Maine and that comfort gave him a second wind. They hadn't stopped for lunch. Calleigh hadn't been hungry and Spencer wasn't too eager to run into another situation like they'd had yesterday at the biker bar.

He stared at himself in the rearview mirror. The black eye had swollen, the pain behind it making friends with the hangover that tormented him. He'd popped some pills mid-way through their drive but even now, they'd worn off.

The Nissan wove through the tree-coated Blue Mountains, catching bits and pieces of the light before it was covered up by a nexus of tree branches. It was another hour before Spencer stopped the car in front of a road leading to a cluster of campgrounds. A small sign nearby read "Welcome to Malheur National Forest."

He pulled the car down the dirt road. The forest floor was coated in a layer of orange pine needles. A cool shadow slid over their car almost like the embrace of an old friend. Moments later, they found themselves at the head of a thronging mass of people.

A collection of vehicles were all parked in a makeshift parking area, packed more tightly than sardines in a can. Spencer could see a few of the big tents that had been set up to welcome visitors just beyond a line of trees down a trail. He squeezed the car into a space between an old Buick station wagon and a mud-slathered Jeep Cherokee.

Calleigh turned to him, beaming for the first time since last night. "We made it!"

"Halle-frickin'-lluja!" he cried, embracing her.

They climbed out each taking a deep breath. The scent of white pine and a distant aroma of grilled food reinvigorated Spencer. The headache was almost forgotten as he slung his bag onto his shoulders and shut the trunk. Almost.

"God, I don't mind if I never see another car seat again, let alone sit in one," he groaned as he rubbed the back of his neck.

Calleigh expertly swatted away a mosquito from her arm. "I couldn't agree more. I almost wouldn't mind if we didn't go back to Maine," she laughed.

Spencer stopped. "Do we have to?"

Calleigh took a few more steps before she turned. "You're serious?"

He moved closer to her. "Calleigh, all I have waiting for me back there is an empty apartment, and a soon-to-be empty office. There's nothing keeping me there anymore."

She perked an eyebrow at him. "Not even your precious Lexus," she joked.

"Eh…maybe."

She rolled her eyes.

"But my point is that I don't want to have to drive back there right away if I don't have to. And something tells me you're not so eager to go back either."

She stared at the ground, kicking the toes of her shoes in the dirt. "You're right. I don't want to *have* to go back. I was holding down a pretty draining job." She brushed a strand of hair out of her face but the breeze blew it back over her forehead. "All I had to look forward to was moving again and having Newton there to make sure the transition went smoothly. But now, he's gone... Best friend that I'd ever had and he's gone."

"Hey," Spencer put his hands on her shoulders and leveled his gaze with hers. "I don't know about you, but I'm tired of this alone crap. I liked what happened last night, I won't lie. It won't matter to me if you look at me as a friend or something more. But I want—need a new beginning. And you're all I have to keep me from going back to who I was."

She took a deep breath, the pain in her face visible.

"Please, don't push me out."

With a force he didn't know Calleigh possessed, she grabbed the collar of his shirt and pulled him closer to her, throwing her arms around him. Spencer held her close, a wholeness repossessing him in a way he'd almost forgotten. The entire journey, it had felt as if there had been a shield up between him and Calleigh. Now with Newton gone, the barrier had fallen. This contact was something totally

190

different, something somehow more pure and invigorating than that kiss they'd shared the night before.

When she pulled away, she smirked, a wild playfulness in her eyes.

He squinted. "What's that look fo—"

SLAP!

Her hand struck his butt with so much force that he leapt forward. "Ah!"

Biting her lip with a grin, she ran up the trailhead away from him. "Well, what are you waiting for? Come and get me!"

Spencer laughed as he took off after her, for the first time in a long time feeling assured that no matter what happened next, he wouldn't have to face it alone.

Thank you for reading

NIGHT TIME, DOTTED LINE

I hope that you enjoyed it and will consider leaving a review on Amazon or Goodreads. I'd appreciate it very much!

Don't forget to visit my websites for news about this book and others!

www.monstrumchronicles.com

http://www.facebook.com/katherinesilva.author

www.themonstrumchronicles.wordpress.com

NIGHT TIME, DOTTED LINE

KATHERINE SILVA

Night Time, Dotted Line Playlist

A compilation of music that inspired the creation of these characters
and their cross-country journey.

Dog Days Are Over: Florence and The Machine

Anything Could Happen: Ellie Goulding

Bedouin Dress: Fleet Foxes

It's Gonna Be: Norah Jones

Be Here Now: Ray LaMontagne

Somebody That I Used To Know: Gotye feat. Kimbra

Long-Legged Guitar Pickin' Man: Johnny Cash and June Carter Cash

Hear Me: Imagine Dragons

Offal Waffle: Little People

Streetwalker: Delta Spirit

Mrs. Cold: Kings of Convenience

Natural Cause: Emancipator

December, 1963 (Oh What A Night!): Frankie Valli and the Four
Seasons

Center of Attention: Guster

A Proper Story: Darren Korb (from Bastion Original Soundtrack)

Big Black Car: Gregory Alan Isakov

The Wolves: Ben Howard

Difficulty: KT Tunstall

VCR: The xx

NIGHT TIME, DOTTED LINE

Enjoy the Ride: Morcheeba

Night Time: The xx

Dear Fellow Traveler: Sea Wolf

Viaje: Austin Wintory (from Journey Music Bundle)

Year of Living Dangerously: Scissor Sisters

A Little Less Conversation (JXL Radio Edit): Elvis Presley

Have You Got It In You?: Imogen Heap

Shadowboxing: Ed Harcourt

Ho Hey: The Lumineers

The Violet Hour: The Civil Wars

Scars On Land: Kings of Convenience

Drive All Night: NEEDTOBREATHE

About the Author

Katherine Silva is the Midcoast Maine author of the speculative fiction series <u>The Monstrum Chronicles</u>, is a connoisseur of coffee, and victim of crazy cat shenanigans. Her most recent novel in the series, <u>Aequitas</u>, was nominated for a 2013 Maine Literary Award. She is a member of the Maine Writers and Publishers Alliance and the New England Horror Writer's Association. <u>Night Time, Dotted Line</u> is her first comedy. Silva lives in Rockland, ME working on the rest of the Monstrum Chronicles as well as other projects.